Jocelyn

W9-CBU-549

Kristy and the Baby Parade

**Other books by
Ann M. Martin**

Ma and Pa Dracula
Yours Turly, Shirley
Ten Kids, No Pets
Slam Book
Just a Summer Romance
Missing Since Monday
With You and Without You
Me and Katie (the Pest)
Stage Fright
Inside Out
Bummer Summer

BABY-SITTERS LITTLE SISTER series
THE BABY-SITTERS CLUB series
(see back of the book for a complete listing)

Kristy and the Baby Parade
Ann M. Martin

AN
APPLE
PAPERBACK

SCHOLASTIC INC.
New York Toronto London Auckland Sydney

Cover art by Hodges Soileau

No part of this publication may be reproduced in whole or in part, or stored in a retrieval system, or transmitted in any form or by any means, electronic, mechanical, photocopying, recording, or otherwise, without written permission of the publisher. For information regarding permission, write to Scholastic Inc., 730 Broadway, New York, NY 10003.

ISBN 0-590-43574-4

Copyright © 1991 by Ann M. Martin. All rights reserved. Published by Scholastic Inc. APPLE PAPERBACKS and THE BABY-SITTERS CLUB are registered trademarks of Scholastic Inc.

12 11 10 9 8 7 6 5 4 3 2 1   1 2 3 4 5 6/9

Printed in the U.S.A.   40

First Scholastic printing, July 1991

The author gratefully acknowledges
Ellen Miles
for her help in
preparing this manuscript.

Kristy and the Baby Parade

CHAPTER 1

O kay, I admit it. I was bored.

I hardly ever get bored while I'm baby-sitting — I love being around kids — but that day was different. It wasn't exactly cold out, but it was kind of gray and dreary. So I'd been indoors all afternoon with David Michael and Emily Michelle. We'd played almost every game in the house at least three times.

"I'm bored!" said David Michael.

"Bowed!" said Emily Michelle. She doesn't speak too well yet, but she can mimic just about anything you say — even if she doesn't have the slightest idea what it means.

Maybe I should back up here and explain a few things, like who I am and why I was sitting for these two bored kids.

I'm Kristy Thomas. I'm thirteen and I'm in the eighth grade at Stoneybrook Middle School. More than anything, I love to baby-sit. In fact, it's kind of a business for me and some of my friends — but I'll tell you more about that later.

It's lucky that I love to baby-sit because I've got a big family that includes quite a few kids who need sitting for. David Michael and Emily Michelle, for example. And then there are Karen and Andrew . . .

Oh, my family's so confusing sometimes. Let me start at the beginning. See, my original family was pretty normal. There were my mom and dad and my two older brothers, Charlie and Sam, me, and my little brother, David Michael.

But just after David Michael was born, my dad walked out on us. He just left. I hear from him now and then, on my birthday (although sometimes he even forgets that) or at Christmas. I think he's living somewhere in California these days. It was hard on us when he first left, but my mom's pretty strong, and she did a great job of holding the family together.

And then, not too long ago, my mom met this really terrific guy named Watson Brewer. They fell in love and got married — so now Watson's my stepfather. After the wedding, we moved across town to live in his mansion.

Watson is a real, true millionaire. Can you believe it? But you'd never know it by the way he acts — he's not stuck up or anything. He's just a regular guy. And he's a great father to his two kids from his first marriage — Karen (she's seven) and Andrew (he's almost five). They live with us every other weekend and for a couple of weeks during the summer. They're terrific kids.

So anyway, once we moved into the mansion, Mom and Watson started to want a baby — and that's where Emily Michelle comes in. When Mom first started talking about a baby, I thought she was planning to get pregnant. But then Watson told us that they were going to adopt a little Vietnamese girl — and that's exactly what they did.

Emily Michelle is two and a half years old, and she's just about the most adorable thing I've ever seen. She doesn't talk much — partly because she's just beginning to understand English. But she's a real sweetie.

David Michael's seven now, and he loves being a big brother. Emily Michelle looks up to him just like I look up to Charlie (he's seventeen) and Sam (he's fifteen).

I haven't even mentioned Nannie yet — she's my grandmother. She moved in with us after we adopted Emily, partly because we needed her help (Mom and Watson both work) and partly because she was tired of living alone. Her husband died years ago.

Nannie's great. She keeps busy and really enjoys life. She has tons of friends, she likes to bowl, and she's always on the go.

There are several other members of my family — but they're not people. We've got a puppy named Shannon — she's a Bernese mountain dog, and she's going to be *huge* some day. And Boo-Boo is Watson's cat. He's old and fat and kind of mean — but he's still part of the family. Plus, Karen and Andrew have two goldfish, Crystal Light the Second and Goldfishie.

So there you have it. I think this is a pretty neat family, even if it is a little complicated.

Now, where was I? Oh, right. I was telling you how bored we all were that day. Well, you'd be bored, too, after playing Clue, Candy Land, Shark Attack (that's Emily's favorite), and one lo-o-ng game of Monopoly.

I racked my brain trying to think of something to do. I wasn't about to turn on the TV — I only do that as a last resort — but I couldn't come up with any other ideas for indoor activities. I kept wishing that the sun would come out so we could go outside, but it refused to budge from behind all those clouds.

Should we make cookies? Nope. Too messy. Mom would be coming home pretty soon, and she'd want to start dinner. Build with Legos? No way. David Michael had told me early in the afternoon that he was sick of Legos.

I got up to put Shark Attack away, and that's

when it hit me. I saw all the magazines and newspapers sitting in their recycling bins on the floor of the hall closet. Collages! We'd make collages.

"Yea!" said David Michael when I told him my idea.

"Yea!"echoed Emily Michelle. I knew that she'd make more of a mess than a work of art, but I knew she'd have fun, too. She loves fooling around with scraps of paper and glue and Magic Markers.

I grabbed a stack of newspapers and magazines and brought them to the kitchen table. Then I got out safety scissors, glue, crayons and markers, and some paper. I sat David Michael and Emily Michelle at the table and told them to go to it.

Pretty soon David Michael was cutting away, his tongue sticking out as he concentrated on not slicing off Darryl Strawberry's head. It only took Emily Michelle about thirty seconds to get glue all over her hands — but I let her go wild, since she was wearing old clothes.

I picked up a recent issue of *Stoneybrook News*, thinking that I might find some interesting things for the two of them to cut out. Most of what I glanced at looked fairly boring, though. There was a long story about the new sewage treatment plant, and another about some people's fiftieth wedding anniversary.

I kept leafing through the paper, looking for good pictures. Then this ad caught my eye. "Calling All Babies!" it said. It was an ad for the Stoneybrook Baby Parade.

The baby parade. I'd forgotten all about it. It's held only once every two years, and I'd never paid much attention to it. I always thought it was kind of silly. It's this big event in which parents dress up their kids in all kinds of wild costumes and try to win prizes. Some of the kids are in strollers, some are in go-carts or wagons, and some are on big floats that hold a whole bunch of kids. There are all these different divisions for different age groups and types of entries.

For example, the ad described Division A, which would include "children in fancy, decorated go-carts, strollers, coaches, or kiddie cars." Division B was for children in *"comic, decorated go-carts, strollers . . ."* You get the picture. Divisions C and D were for floats of various sizes.

There would be a grand marshall for the parade, and judges who would pick first-, second-, and third-place winners in each division. All children under the age of three were eligible to enter. The ad said to watch for applications.

I remembered some of the baby parades I'd

seen. They were pretty crazy! Every entry has to have a "theme" — and some of the themes are kind of . . . well, imaginative. Like the float one year that was called "Circus Days." It featured a twelve-foot-high elephant on wheels! Or the "Wild West" float I saw once, with a cowboys-and-Indians pageant being acted out on top of it.

Babies in strollers had to have themes, too — they might be dressed up like fairy-tale characters or people in the movies.

It was pretty silly, all right.

But after I'd read that ad, my glance kept resting on Emily Michelle. She's adorable. Did I already tell you that? Well, she is. I looked at her glossy, straight black hair cut like a Dutch girl's. I looked at her sparkling brown almond-shaped eyes. I looked at her plump, pink cheeks and at her sturdy little hands (all covered with glue at the moment, but still very cute) and at her round little tummy.

I was getting an idea.

I'm famous for that — getting ideas, that is. Just ask my friends. I don't mean to sound egotistical or anything. It's just something I'm good at. Ideas pop into my head, and a lot of them turn out to be pretty terrific.

I'm sure you can guess what this idea was about. That's right. I was thinking of entering Emily in the baby parade. She'd be bound to win a prize — and it would be so much fun to dress her up and show her off.

I looked at her some more. What division would I enter her in? What kind of costume should she have? There was a lot to think about.

"Do you like my collage, Kristy?" asked David Michael suddenly. I shook myself. I'd been thinking so hard that I'd forgotten what we were doing. I looked at David Michael's creation.

"That's great!" I said. And it was, kind of. It had a baseball theme — that is, David Michael had cut out every picture he could find that had anything to do with baseball, and then he'd pasted them all onto a piece of paper, in no particular order. It was about four layers thick, and pictures were hanging off the sides. He'd also cut out words like HOME RUN and RED SOX from headlines. Those were pasted right over the pictures.

"Charlie'll love it," I said. I knew he would, too. He loves anything that has to do with baseball.

Just then, I heard the front door slam. "Anybody home?" called a voice.

"There's Charlie now!" I said. "That means Mom will be home soon, too. Time to clean up." I looked at the mess Emily Michelle had made, and I sighed. She might be perfect-looking, but she's just like any other two-and-a-half-year-old when it comes down to it.

I helped clear off the table, thinking all the time about the baby parade. Soon Sam came home, and then Nannie got back from bowling practice, and right on her heels were Mom and Watson.

Before long, the house was full of noise and activity as we all helped get dinner ready. As I told you earlier, I love my wild family. But that night, I was glad when dinner was over and I could go up to my nice quiet room to start my homework — and think about my latest idea.

I was sure that my friends would be excited about the baby parade, too. Maybe Jessi would want to enter Squirt! And there are lots of other babies whom we sit for. This could be a great activity for the whole club!

What club?

Oh, I guess I haven't told you about it yet. Well, it's a long story.

CHAPTER 2

The club I've been talking about is special. It's special because it's more than a club — it's a business, as I mentioned before. It's also special because of the people who belong to it. There are seven of us in the Baby-sitters Club, and I consider each one of the other members my good friend.

Sometimes, I think it's amazing that we're all such close friends — because we're very different. Of course, we do have things in common. We love to baby-sit, for one. That's probably why the club works so well.

I'm the president of the BSC. That's because it was my idea. (Remember how I said that I often have good ideas? Well, this one was the best ever.) I try to run the club in a businesslike way, and I know that sometimes it means I come across as a little bossy. But my friends put up with it pretty well.

They're used to me. They're used to the fact that I have (I admit it) a big mouth. It's not that I'm *mean* or anything, but I'm not always as tactful as I could be. They're also used to the fact that I'm not as sophisticated as the rest of them: I'm not interested in clothes (I usually dress for comfort, not for style — which means jeans, a turtleneck, and running shoes most days) or makeup or any of that stuff.

Boys? Well, until recently I wasn't interested at all. But lately I've developed a crush on this guy Bart, who coaches a softball team in my neighborhood. I coach one, too. His team's name is Bart's Bashers, and mine is called Kristy's Krushers.

But you know what? I don't think I'm ready for a real boyfriend. Not after seeing what my best friend, Mary Anne Spier, went through with her boyfriend, Logan Bruno.

We all thought they were the perfect couple — but then they broke up. The breakup was kind of Mary Anne's idea, but it was tough on her just the same.

Mary Anne's a truly sensitive person. She's romantic and a good listener and she cries very, very easily. You might think that would mean that she and I wouldn't get along all that well, since I don't seem to have a sensitive

11

bone in my body. Somehow, though, our friendship has survived my big mouth.

Though we're different in terms of personality, we're alike in other ways. For example, looks. We're both short for our age (actually, I'm even shorter than Mary Anne. I'm the shortest girl in my grade) and have brown hair and brown eyes. Mary Anne tends to dress a little more stylishly than I do — there are times when she actually looks cool, which I *never* do.

We've been friends forever — or at least it seems that way. I used to live right next door to her, before Mom and Watson got married. Mary Anne's mom died when Mary Anne was just a baby, and her dad brought her up all by himself.

Mr. Spier tried really hard to be a good father. In fact, maybe he tried *too* hard. For years, he was incredibly strict with Mary Anne. There were all kinds of rules she had to follow, and she could only dress a certain way. It used to drive her crazy. But finally Mr. Spier started to loosen up. He didn't even seem to mind that Mary Anne had a boyfriend! (She's the only one in our club who has had one, by the way.)

Mr. Spier actually loosened up so much that he started dating this woman who happened to be his old high-school sweetheart. She also happened to be the mother of one of our other club members, Dawn Schafer!

See, Dawn's mom had grown up in Stoneybrook, but then she got married and moved to California. Years later, she got divorced, and she and Dawn (and Dawn's younger brother, Jeff) moved back to Stoneybrook. And after she and Mr. Spier had dated for awhile, they decided to get married!

So Mary Anne's *other* best friend, Dawn, is now also her stepsister. Mary Anne and her dad (and her kitten, Tigger, too) moved into Dawn's house to live with Dawn and her mom.

What about Jeff? Well, he missed his dad — and California — so much that he moved back there. Now Dawn misses *him*, but she knows he made the right decision.

I think Dawn's happy here in Stoneybrook. I know she misses the sunny beaches and the more laid-back life-style of California, but she's adjusted well to life in Connecticut. Dawn *looks* like my idea of a California girl, though. She's a real knockout, with her blue eyes and her long, long, pale blonde hair. She's got a style all her own, too — my friends and I call it "California casual." She wears lots of cool clothes in bright colors.

By the way, Dawn was always pretty, even as a little kid. She once told me that when she was two years old, her mom entered her picture in a baby contest — and she won first prize!

But Dawn's not at all stuck-up. I don't even think she has any idea how pretty she is. Dawn is — well, she's mellow, that's the only way I can describe her. She does her own thing, and doesn't care much what other people think of her. I admire her for that.

She's been through some pretty rocky times — first her parents' divorce, and then her brother moving back to California, and then her mom's remarriage. (Even though Dawn and Mary Anne are best friends, it took some time for them to adjust to being in the same family.) But she's hung in there throughout all of it, even when the rest of us knew she must be hurting.

One of Dawn's favorite things about Stoneybrook is the house she lives in. Dawn loves to read ghost stories — so what could be better for her than living in a haunted house? You might think I'm kidding, but I'm not. The house is really, really old, and it has a secret passage. We're almost sure that a ghost lives there!

And if it does, maybe Dawn and Claudia can catch it. Claudia Kishi is another member of our club, and her favorite reading consists of Nancy Drew mysteries. She considers herself a pretty good detective.

Claudia is just as gorgeous as Dawn, but in a totally different way. Instead of pale blonde hair, Claudia's is jet-black. Instead of blue eyes, Claudia's got beautiful brown almond-shaped ones.

Claudia is Japanese-American — very exotic and very, very cool. If you want to talk about style, you've got to talk about Claudia Kishi. Nobody in Stoneybrook can put together a wild outfit like Claud can. She's always up on the latest trend, whether it's big black shoes, tie-dyed leggings, or cool hats.

Her parents don't mind the way she dresses (though they'd probably draw the line if she wanted to dye her hair green or get a Mohawk or something) because they know it's all part of Claudia's artistic sense, which they like to encourage.

See, Claud's not a great student — not because she's dumb, but because she's just not that interested in school. (Her older sister, Janine, *loves* school — she's a certified genius, so that would explain it.) But Claudia's less-than-average grades in English and math are balanced out by her above-average artistic talent.

Painting, drawing, sculpting — you name it, Claudia's terrific at it. You wouldn't believe the beautiful things she's made. She even makes her own jewelry sometimes — which just adds to her distinctive personal style.

I mentioned that Claud's parents encourage her artistic talent, but did I tell you how they feel about her passion for Nancy Drew books? Well, they don't exactly approve, so Claud has to hide her books. She's good at hiding things, because she's got another habit her parents disapprove of: eating junk food.

Now, I like to have an occasional Twinkie as much as the next person, and I won't turn down a Kit-Kat bar. But Claudia is on another level of junk-food eating altogether. Security for Claud would be knowing that there are some M&M's in her sock drawer, a pack of Yodels in her paint box, and a bag of that new kind of Doritos — the ones with extra cheese? — on the top shelf of her closet.

The funny thing is that even though Claudia is a very generous person, she can't share her junk food with her best friend, Stacey McGill. Why not? Well, the reason isn't all that funny. It's because Stacey has diabetes, a disease in which her blood sugar can get out of whack, and she has to be very, very careful about what she eats.

Not too long ago, Stacey got really sick — partly because she had gone off her strict no-sugar diet, and partly because her blood sugar had gotten really hard to control. She was in the hospital and everything, and we were all pretty worried about her. But she's fine now. And I think she will be, as long as she takes care of herself. ("Taking care of herself" includes giving herself daily injections of this stuff called insulin, which her body doesn't make anymore. Giving yourself shots! Can you imagine? Ew.)

Stacey hasn't lived in Stoneybrook for that long, even though we all feel like we've known her forever. She grew up in New York City — and she's just as sophisticated as you might imagine. Sometimes she and Claudia decide to get really dressed up. They try their best to outdo each other with wild hairdos (Stacey has blonde hair that she gets permed once in awhile), crazy earrings, and the coolest clothes this side of the Connecticut state line.

Stacey stays in touch with what's happening in the city because her father lives there and she visits him fairly often. That's right, Stacey's parents are divorced, too. And the split took place pretty recently.

What happened was this. Stacey's family first moved to Stoneybrook when she was in seventh grade because her dad got transferred to his company's Stamford office. (That's a city near here.) Then, just when we'd made friends with her, he got transferred back to New York and the McGills had to move back there! We were so sad to see Stacey go.

But pretty soon after they'd returned to the city, Stacey's parents began to fight a lot, and finally they chose to separate. Her mom decided to move back to Stoneybrook, and we were all thrilled when Stacey (who was given the choice of coming back here or living with her dad in his city apartment) came with her.

Let's see. Me, Mary Anne, Dawn, Claudia, Stacey . . . There are still two other members of the BSC that I haven't told you about. Jessi and Mallory are younger than the rest of us — they're eleven and in sixth grade at Stoneybrook Middle School. (All of the rest of us are thirteen and in eighth grade.)

Jessi Ramsey's family has only lived in Stoneybrook for a little while. They bought the house that Stacey used to live in! And when they moved in, they caused a bit of a stir in the neighborhood. Why? Because they're black. Big deal, right? That's what all of us thought. But a lot of people felt differently. There aren't too many black families in Stoneybrook — and some people wanted it to stay that way.

But you know what? Most people accept the

Ramseys now. They're a great family. Jessi's the oldest of three kids: She's got a little sister named Becca, who's eight, and the cutest baby brother named Squirt. (Well, he wasn't actually *named* Squirt — that's just his nickname. His real name is John Philip Ramsey, Jr.)

Mallory Pike is the oldest in her family, too. But her family is a *lot* bigger than Jessi's. Mal has four brothers and three sisters! (Three of her brothers are triplets.)

Being the oldest is sometimes hard on Mal and Jessi — mainly because they feel that while they have lots of responsibilities, they still get treated like babies by their parents. You know how it is when you're eleven. You want to be treated like more of a grown-up, but your parents still see you as a kid. Jessi and Mal did win one round with their parents: They were finally allowed to get their ears pierced. But Mal still has braces *and* glasses. Oh, well.

Like any best friends, Jessi and Mal have a lot in common (they both love to read horse stories, for example). But they also have a lot of separate interests. Jessi loves to dance — I'm sure she'll be a professional ballerina some day, if she wants to be. She's really, really talented. And Mal is a writer and an artist. She's always keeping journals and sketching and making up stories. She wants to write — and illustrate — children's books when she's older.

So, those are the members of the BSC. I'm sure you can see why I think our club is pretty special — and why I consider myself so lucky to have such a great group of friends.

CHAPTER 3

Claudia's room. Monday, 5:25 P.M. If that's the time and place, you can bet what kind of mood I'll be in. I'll be feeling great, because it's almost time for the first BSC meeting of the week.

That day was no exception. I sat in Claudia's director's chair, wearing my visor. (I always wear my visor during meetings; it makes me feel more official.) I had tucked a pencil over my ear, and I was watching the clock, waiting for the others to arrive.

I'm almost always the first club member to reach Claud's room. Why? Because I'm the president, and I feel it's my responsibility to start the meeting on time.

We've run the club in a businesslike way, right from the start. I think it's part of the reason that we've been so successful. Who could have guessed that such a simple idea would have turned out so well? As I sat and waited that day, I thought back to the very beginning of the club. . . .

It was the beginning of seventh grade. I was still living next door to Mary Anne, and across the street from Claudia, on Bradford Court. Mom and Watson were dating, but I had no idea that they'd end up married.

Even back then, I loved to baby-sit. But the person I sat for most was my own brother, David Michael. He needed watching every day after school until Mom got home from work. I also sat for him in the evening sometimes, when Mom went out with Watson.

Sam and Charlie watched David Michael, too, — so it was rare that Mom had to hire a baby-sitter from outside the family. But once in awhile everybody wanted to go out at the same time. One afternoon Mom realized that she'd need to hire a sitter for the next day. She got on the phone and started calling around, looking for somebody to bail us out. I'll never forget that night. We were eating pizza and Mom's got cold while she kept making calls.

That's when I got this idea. What if Mom could call just one number that would put her in touch with a whole bunch of experienced baby-sitters? One of them would *have* to be free. I got really excited about it, and I told Mary Anne and Claudia as soon as I could.

What if, I asked them, we formed a club that would meet a few times a week? During those times, parents could call us to line up sitters.

They thought it was a great idea, but Claud pointed out (and Mary Anne agreed) that three people weren't going to be enough to keep up with the demand for sitters. Claud had just met — and made friends with — Stacey, so we asked her to join, too. By the time Dawn moved to Stoneybrook, we had so much business that we were nearly desperate for another member. So Dawn joined the club.

How did Jessi and Mal get to be members? Well, remember how I told you that Stacey's family moved back to New York for awhile, right before her parents got the divorce? When she left, the club just couldn't keep up with all its sitting jobs, so that's when Jessi and Mal joined. Of course, when Stacey came back, she was automatically part of the club again.

The club seems to be just about the right size now, especially since we also have two associate members, Shannon and Logan. (I'll tell you more about them later.) They don't come to meetings (there's no way *nine* of us could fit comfortably into Claud's room), but they help us out when we need extra sitters.

You might be wondering how we get all this business I keep talking about. Well, some of it is "word of mouth." Parents we've sat for have been impressed with us and have told other parents to call us. Also, we advertise. We made up these cool-looking fliers (Claud designed them), and every now and then we distribute them around the neighborhood. Once we even put an ad in the *Stoneybrook News* — but we haven't had to do that again. We have as much business as we can handle.

The fliers explain how the club works. We meet every Monday, Wednesday, and Friday from 5:30 to 6:00, and parents can call us then to line up a sitter. Parents love knowing they'll find a sitter, and we love to baby-sit!

I told you that I'm the president, but I haven't explained what everybody else in the club does. This is one club where every member has a job or a position.

Claudia is the vice-president. She doesn't exactly have a job to do, but she's vice-president for a few good reasons. First of all, we meet in her bedroom. Why? Because she's the only member who has her own phone — and her own private line. We could never tie up any grown-ups' lines with all the calls we get during our meetings.

Claud also might be referred to as the re-freshment officer, if there were such a thing. She's very generous with her junk food. As soon as each meeting gets under way, Claudia digs out the snacks. She's thoughtful, too. She knows that Stacey and Dawn don't go for junk food (Stacey because of her diabetes; Dawn because she's addicted to health food) so she always makes sure to have some plain, boring thing like whole-wheat pretzels on hand, to supplement the Ring-Dings and Pringle's potato chips.

Mary Anne is our club secretary. What a job she has! She keeps track of all our appointments in this big notebook that we call the club record book. The information in that book is irreplaceable. The record book has all the names and addresses of our clients (as well as special facts about their pets, their children's allergies, and other stuff). It also includes our sitting appointments.

Mary Anne has another important task. She has to keep track of all our schedules. That might sound simple, but when you start to think about the things we do — Jessi's dance classes, my softball practices, Claud's art classes, Mallory's orthodonist appointments — well, you get the picture. When a call comes in from a parent looking for a sitter, Mary Anne can tell at a glance which of us is free. She's never made a mistake, which is pretty awesome.

Stacey, the math whiz, is our treasurer. She keeps track of how much money we earn (even though we each keep what we make, we like to know the total), and she also collects our dues every Monday. We *hate* giving up any of our hard-earned money, but we know it's going to a good cause.

Or several good causes, that is. For example, we use some of the money to pay my brother Charlie to drive me to meetings, since I now live so far from Claud's house. And some of it goes toward Claud's phone bill. And once in awhile, we get crazy and spend some on a big pizza blowout.

Dawn is our alternate officer. That means that she knows how to do all our jobs, so we're covered if anybody has to miss a meeting. She was terrific as treasurer, for example, during the time that Stacey had moved back to New York.

Mallory and Jessi are our junior officers. Since they're younger, they don't sit alone at night. But they handle a lot of our afternoon and weekend jobs, which is a tremendous help.

Last but not least are our associate members, the ones I told you about who don't come to meetings. One of them is Shannon Kilbourne, this girl who lives in my new neighborhood. The other is Logan Bruno. Does that name sound familiar? That's right, he's Mary Anne's "ex." He's a good sitter, too. I'm glad we have him and Shannon to fall back on when the rest of us are too busy to take a job.

"Hey, Kristy, aren't you going to call the meeting to order?"

I snapped my head around to see who had spoken. It was Stacey. She sat in Claud's desk chair, grinning at me and pointing at the digital clock. Its big, white numbers said 5:31. I'd been lost in my thoughts and had almost forgotten that it was my job to get things going.

"Thanks, Stacey!" I said. Then I sat up straight, pulled the pencil out from behind my ear, and tapped it on the arm of my chair. "Order!" I said. "This meeting will now come to order!"

Everybody looked at me and giggled. "We've been *wondering* when you'd get around to starting the meeting," said Claudia, who was sitting on the bed between Dawn and Mary Anne. She tore open a bag of barbecue potato chips and passed it to Jessi and Mallory, who were in their usual places on the floor.

"Any club business?" I asked, looking around the room. Stacey held up the manila envelope that we keep our dues in. "Oh, right," I said. "It's Monday. Okay, everybody, pay up!" We groaned as Stacey passed the envelope around, but we all chipped in.

"Hey, Stacey," said Dawn as the envelope went around. "Do we have enough money for some new stickers? My Kid-Kit is all out of them."

I don't want to sound conceited, but Kid-Kits are another of my great ideas. I noticed something once when David Michael had some friends over. Kids sometimes like to play with *other* kids' toys more than their own. So I thought that we could each make up a kit to take with us on sitting jobs. They're boxes we've decorated with glitter and stuff, and they're full of toys and books and stickers and games.

The kids just love our Kid-Kits, especially on rainy days. And when the kids are happy, the parents are happy, and when the parents are happy, they hire us again. Then we're happy! It's very simple.

Stacey doled out some money to Dawn, and to Mallory, who said she needed crayons for *her* Kid-Kit. Stacey frowned as she counted out the change, and I had to stifle a giggle. She's a great treasurer partly because she *hates* to spend our money.

"Okay," I said. "While we're waiting for the phone to ring — " and just then, it did. I almost jumped out of my seat, but I recovered in time to make a grab for it. It was Mrs.

Perkins, one of our regular clients. She wanted a sitter for that Thursday, and I said I'd call her back. Mary Anne checked the record book and said that Claud was the only one free, so Claud got the job. Once I'd called back Mrs. Perkins, I started over again.

"Has everyone read the club notebook?" I asked. There were nods all around the room. The club notebook is another of my ideas, and I have to admit that it's not one of my most popular ones. The notebook is where we write up each of our sitting jobs, giving all the gory details so that the other club members can keep up-to-date on what's happening with our clients. Everybody's pretty good about reading the entries, but nobody (except Mal, maybe) really likes to write them. It takes time, but I have to say that it's worth it. I think it helps us to be better sitters.

"I liked what Dawn had to say about her new technique for dealing with temper tantrums," said Mary Anne. "I never would have thought of tucking children into their beds and talking gently to them until they felt calmer."

"It really works, too!" said Dawn.

We talked some more about "tantrum techniques," and then I started to tell the others about the baby parade. But just then, the phone rang again and Stacey grabbed it. She rolled her eyes when she first heard who was calling, so we all knew it had to be Mrs. Prezzioso, one of our more "difficult" clients. Then she listened for a long time, saying an occasional "yes" and "I see."

I was dying to know what the call was about. Finally, Stacey said she'd call Mrs. Prezzioso back and hung up.

"What did she want?" I asked.

Stacey filled us in. It seemed that Mrs. Prezzioso was looking for a regular sitter — two afternoons a week — for a whole month. The Prezziosos have two daughters: Jenny, who's three, and can be kind of a brat, and Andrea, who's a baby.

"Mrs. P.'s going to be on the planning board at Jenny's preschool, and she needs a babysitter for when she has to go to meetings," said Stacey.

"What's so complicated about that?" I asked.

"Well, here's the thing. She said that since Andrea is a little more active and alert now — she's not a newborn anymore, you know — she would want the sitter to have taken an infant-care class. She said one's about to start at the community center, and she'll pay the fee for it."

"I'd *love* to do that!" I said right away. I'm always up for learning more about how to be a good baby-sitter.

"Well, that's good," said Mary Anne. "Because you're the only one of us who could take the job." She'd been checking the schedule, and I guess everybody else had conflicts because of classes and things. "But you know what?" she added. "I think I'd like to take that class, too. I've seen the ads for it, and it looks like fun."

"I wouldn't mind learning more about babies, myself," said Claud. "What if we all sign up for the course? Then we could advertise ourselves as 'infant specialists'! Maybe we'd get some new business."

Wow. That was a great idea — the kind *I* usually had. I tried not to be jealous. "Sounds great!" I said. And by the end of the meeting, we'd called the community center to sign up. All seven of us.

CHAPTER 4

"Oh, wow!" Mary Anne stood looking around the room, her hand over her mouth. We had gotten to the community center early — I guess we were eager to see what the infant-care classes would be like.

"Mary Anne!" I hissed, elbowing her. "Quit staring! You've seen pregnant women before."

"Yeah, but only one at a time," she whispered. "A whole room full of them is different. It's kind of — "

"Overwhelming?" asked a friendly voice. A red-haired woman had appeared next to me, and she was smiling at us. "I know. I've been teaching this course for three years now, and I'm still not used to it."

We stood for a moment, taking in the sight of all those round women. They stood in groups, talking and laughing. There were also a few men there — I guess they were fathersto-be. Some of them were discussing a poster that was hung on the front wall: DIAPERING TECHNIQUES, it said, and it listed all the dos and don'ts of diapering. It looked like a long list.

I also saw a cluster of parents with young babies in their arms. They seemed to have a lot to talk about with each other.

"You must be the girls who have the club," said the red-haired woman. "I'm Anita. I'm glad you decided to take the course — more baby-sitters should, but a lot don't want to spend the time."

"I wanted to take it as soon as I heard about it," said Mary Anne. "My name's Mary Anne Spier, by the way. And this is my best friend, Kristy Thomas. She's the president of The Baby-sitters Club."

I could hardly believe my ears. Mary Anne is usually shy! It must have been Anita's friendly smile that made her feel comfortable so quickly.

"The other members of our club should be here soon," I said. "We're pretty excited about the class. Oh, look!" I pointed to the doorway. A woman had just come in, and she was carrying not one, but two small babies.

"That's Mrs. Salem," said Anita. "She had twins a few months ago. Aren't they darling? Come on, I'll introduce you."

"So this class is for new parents *and* expectant parents?" I asked.

"That's right," said Anita. "And for anybody else who wants to learn more about taking care of babies." She led us across the room. "Liz, meet Kristy and Mary Anne," she said. "Girls, this is Mrs. Salem."

Mrs. Salem smiled at us. She looked kind of tired. She had set both of the babies on a table, in infant seats. "Hi! I like your T-shirts. Do you really belong to a baby-sitters club?"

I looked down. I'd almost forgotten that we'd decided to wear our club T-shirts to class. "Yes, we do." I said. "We've been in business for awhile now, and we decided that it was time to learn a little more about babies. Your twins are adorable! What are their names?"

"This is Ricky," she said, folding back a soft yellow blanket from one of the babies' faces. "He's the troublemaker. And this," she said stroking the face of the other one, "is Rose. She's no angel, either."

They were both so, so cute. When Mary Anne held her finger out to Ricky, he grabbed onto it with his tiny hand and wouldn't let go. Mary Anne squealed. "He's so strong!" she said.

Mrs. Salem laughed. "I know. And Rose has got an even tighter grip!"

"Hi, you guys," said Stacey, coming up behind us. "Oh, how cute!" She and Claudia bent over the twins, cooing. Dawn appeared a minute later and joined them.

"Okay, people!" said Anita, clapping her hands. "Let's get started. I'd like everybody to take a seat, and we'll spend a few minutes getting to know each other."

Just as we were sitting down in the small circle of chairs at the front of the room, Jessi and Mal arrived. Jessi slipped into the chair next to me. "Are we late?" she whispered.

"No," I answered. "You're just in time."

"Oh, good," she said. "We got stuck in traffic after my dad picked me up from ballet class. For awhile I thought we weren't going to make it."

"Okay," said Anita, once we were settled. "Let's just go around the circle and introduce ourselves. I'd like each of you to say your first name and a few words about why you're here. I'm Anita, and this is my partner, Don," she said, gesturing to a man sitting next to her.

He was really handsome.

He was wearing glasses, and he was kind of old — not as old as Watson, but maybe the same age as my English teacher, Mr. Fiske. I tried not to stare at him as he smiled at us and said hi.

The first person to speak was a cheerful-looking dark-haired woman. "I'm Sue," she said. "This is my husband, John." She pointed to a bearded man sitting next to her. "And I guess it's pretty obvious why we're taking this class." She patted her belly and giggled. "Junior, here, is going to be arriving soon, and we don't have the slightest idea of how to take care of him. I've brought up plenty of puppies, but I have a feeling that's not quite the same thing."

Anita smiled. "You're right. For example, you don't have to worry about a baby chewing up your best pair of shoes!"

We laughed. If any of us had been feeling shy before, the ice was broken now. The introductions continued. I noticed a lot of interest when we told the group about our club, which made me realize that we were probably meeting a bunch of potential clients. I hadn't thought of that before. This class was going to be great for the club in more ways than one.

"Welcome all," said Anita. "Now let's get down to work." She turned to the blackboard and wrote out a list of topics we'd be covering in class. "Child Development: Birth to Six Months," the list began. And then, "What Babies Do . . . and Don't Do; Feeding; Diapering; Bathing; Sleep Schedules; and Playtime."

"This looks like a lot, I know," said Anita. "But we'll take it bit by bit, and by the end of the course, you'll all be baby experts."

"Diapering is the worst part!" whispered Mary Anne. "I can never figure out how to do it without making a big mess with the powder and everything."

"It just takes some practice," I whispered back.

Anita was passing out some pamphlets. "I think you'll find these helpful," she said. "They contain lots of good information. Now let's talk about babies," she went on. "One of the most important things to remember is that babies are totally dependent on you for their care. But they can't tell you what they need or want — all they can do is cry, and it's up to you to figure out what's wrong."

As if on cue, Ricky — or maybe it was Rose — began to wail. Loudly. Mrs. Salem picked the baby up and held it. She looked a little embarrassed.

"That's okay, Liz. Let's just take this as an example. What do you think the baby wants?"

"It's Ricky," said Mrs. Salem. "And that sounds like his 'I'm hungry' cry. But there's only one way to find out for sure." She pulled a bottle out of the bag by her feet and offered it to Ricky. He turned his head away and kept screaming.

"I guess that wasn't it," said Mrs. Salem. "Maybe he's just restless. Sometimes he likes to be walked around the room. I think he gets tired of looking at the same scenery for too long." She stood up, still holding him. "Could somebody keep an eye on Rose?" she asked.

"I'll watch her," I said.

Mrs. Salem started walking, jiggling Ricky a little with each step, and talking to him in a soothing voice. But it didn't take too many laps around the room for all of us to figure out that a change of scene wasn't going to be the answer. Ricky just kept on yelling his head off.

"I'm so sorry," said Mrs. Salem. Now she looked *really* embarrassed. She jiggled Ricky some more, and said, "Come on, buddy. What's the matter? It's okay," in a soft voice.

He wouldn't stop crying.

"Don't worry, Liz — we'll just make a lesson out of this," said Anita, smiling. "What else might Ricky want? Does anybody have any ideas?"

"Maybe he want a favorite toy to play with," said one of the pregnant women.

"Well," said Anita, "that's a possibility. But he's so young it's not likely that he's attached to any one toy. Right now, he's mainly interested in being held, and in eating — basic things like that. Anybody else?"

Ricky was still sobbing.

"I can't take it!" I heard Claud whisper to

Stacey. "How much longer do you think he'll cry?"

Stacey giggled. "I never knew that such a little thing could make so much noise," she whispered back.

"He's not colicky, is he?" asked Don, who had stood up and walked over to where Mrs. Salem was standing.

"Oh, no," said Mrs. Salem. "I can't imagine how I would cope if he was."

"What's 'colicky'?" asked Jessi.

"That's when babies have trouble with their digestion, and they get terrible stomach-aches," said Don. "Nobody really knows why it happens to some babies, but when it does, they can cry for three or four hours at a time."

"Oh, my lord!" said Claudia.

"But what can you do when they're like that?" asked Dawn.

"Not much," said Don. "It can be really hard on the parents. All they can do is walk the baby around and try to comfort it."

I hope I never have to sit for a baby with colic.

All this time, Ricky had still been screaming his head off. Suddenly, I had an idea. I caught Anita's eye and said, "Do you think he needs a clean diaper?"

"Good idea, Kristy," she said. "What do you think, Liz?"

"That could be it," said Mrs. Salem. "He tends to be really bothered by a wet diaper. Rose doesn't seem to care."

"Let's try it," said Anita. She brought Mrs. Salem's diaper bag over to the changing table that had been set up in the front of the room. Mrs. Salem put Ricky down on the table, and his screams grew even louder. Everybody gathered around to watch. Luckily, I was close enough to see well and still be able to keep an eye on Rose.

"Oh, you use cloth diapers," said Anita. "Great. We need to learn how to put on both kinds, disposable and cloth. So many parents are switching to cloth these days. They are much better for the environment, if you're willing to do just a little more work."

Anita changed Ricky's diaper, talking the whole time about what she was doing. And by the time he was clean and dry, his sobs had died down and he was happily blowing bubbles and making gurgling noises.

I could see that this class was going to be a challenge—and a lot of fun.

CHAPTER 5

"This is our son, Ethan," said Anita. She put her arm around a little boy with strawberry-blond hair. He was wearing a T-shirt with a big purple dinosaur on it.

"Hi, Ethan," I said. "I like your shirt!"

"Say hello to Kristy, Ethan," said Don.

But Ethan was feeling a little bit shy. He rubbed one of his sneakered toes against the other and pressed his face into Don's leg.

"That's okay," I said. "Sometimes I feel shy, too." What a cute kid! I'd gotten used to the idea that Anita and Don were married — that had become clear by the end of the first class. After four weeks, I still had kind of a crush on Don; so did Stacey and Dawn — in fact, I think all of us BSC members thought he was pretty terrific.

But I hadn't met Ethan before, so this was something new. All at once I saw Don in a different light: He was just another father, someone who would hire me as a baby-sitter, tell me where the plunger was in case the plumbing backed up, and go out to the movies with his wife. My crush disappeared. Just like that. I still liked him, but I was no longer "infatuated," as Mary Anne had put it.

I was pretty dressed up that Saturday afternoon. I'd worn a skirt with my turtleneck instead of my usual jeans. Why? Because the class was over, and we were about to "graduate." We would each be getting a certificate that said we had passed the infant-care course.

We'd been told that we could invite people to the ceremony, so the room was pretty full. Kids were running around and screaming, and lots of people were talking and laughing.

Mom and Watson hadn't been able to come, but Nannie and Charlie were there. Our associate members, Shannon and Logan, had come, and I was happy to see Logan and Mary Anne together again.

It must be hard to learn how to be friends with someone you used to go out with.

Claudia's parents and her sister, Janine, were there, and so was Stacey's mom. Dawn's mom and Mary Anne's dad sat together, looking around the room and smiling at the way the kids were playing together.

Jessi's little sister, Becca, was the only member of the Ramsey family who could come. She had gotten a ride with the Pikes, who had turned out in full force.

I was feeling a little nervous about the graduation ceremony. Why? Well, because we had taken some tests the week before, and we were about to find out how we'd done on them. Anita had said that we had all passed, so it wasn't that I was worried about failing. It was just that I was really hoping I had done well on the tests. I'd enjoyed the course, and I felt it was important to demonstrate that I'd learned something from it.

I should say that the tests we took weren't called "tests" by Anita and Don. They called them "evaluations," and they warned us not to take them too seriously.

"These evaluations are just to help us be sure you've learned everything you should have from the course," Don had said.

Even though they weren't supposed to matter so much, I did take the tests seriously.

The first one had been a written "evaluation" — a series of questions, mostly multiple-choice.

Here's an example of one of the questions:

You are changing a diaper for six-month-old Rebecca when you hear the phone ringing in the next room. What do you do?

A) Run to answer it. The call could be important, and Rebecca's comfortable on the changing table. She'll wait.

B) Grab Rebecca and make a run for the phone. You might still get there before it stops ringing.

C) Let it ring. You can't leave Rebecca alone on the changing table.

That one was easy. C, of course. But some of the other questions were a little harder. When I finished that test (I mean, evaluation) I thought I'd done pretty well. But there were one or two questions I wasn't so sure about.

Mary Anne and I talked afterward, comparing answers. She'd had a much harder time with the test than I had — maybe because she grew up as an only child and never had the day-to-day experience with younger kids I'd had, first with David Michael and now with Emily.

The other evaluation had covered what Anita called "practical skills." For that, we'd each had to demonstrate that we'd learned how to do certain things. For example, we had to put a diaper on a doll, following all the steps we had been taught. Then we had to clean the "baby," put on some cornstarch-based powder (the old kind, talcum, isn't so good for babies), and fasten the diaper securely — all while pretending that the 'baby' was real.

Anita and Don watched closely. They'd told us that they would be taking points off for things like squeezing powder straight from the container — we were supposed to shake it into our hands first, so that we wouldn't risk shooting powder into the baby's face. We also had to make sure to keep one hand on the baby at all times, since they'd told us that it only takes a second for a baby to roll off a changing table.

We also had to show that we knew at least three ways to hold a baby safely, and that we knew where the soft spot is on a baby's head. Plus, we had to demonstrate our burping technique. All of this was done using dolls to stand in for real babies.

I'd been so nervous while I was diapering the doll that I honestly wasn't sure whether I'd done everything right. We'd been tested with cloth diapers, because they were harder to use. Had I slipped my hand under the diaper when I pinned it, so that I wouldn't stick the baby? Had I remembered to fold the diaper right?

Oh, well. I'd find out soon enough.

"Can we get started?"

I heard Anita talking at the front of the room, but a lot of other people didn't. The noise level was still pretty high.

"Attention, all graduates!" boomed Don above the racket. "Do any of you want your certificates?"

That seemed to do it. The hubbub died down, and everybody took a few minutes to find seats and settle in for the ceremony.

"We're very proud of you," said Anita. "Remember when I told you that you'd be baby experts by the end of the course? Well, I'd have to say that all of you have reached that goal."

"But," said Don, "there were only two people in the class who got every answer correct on their written evaluations and who also got top scores on the practical section."

I leaned forward to hear what he would say next. I didn't even dare to hope that I could be one of those people. I took a quick look around the room, trying to guess who they might be. I noticed one woman who was due to give birth that very day — Mrs. Nielsen. She'd been very good at diapering, I remembered. And I knew that Dawn had definitely aced the practical part of the evaluation. I'd watched her, and she'd done everything perfectly.

"The first person with a perfect score is John Davenport. Can you come up and get your certificate, John?" That was a surprise! Anita smiled at the bearded man who walked up and shook her hand. "Good work, John! You're the first man in any of our classes who has gotten a perfect score."

"And the other person," said Don, "is one of our younger students."

Dawn! I knew it.

"Kristy Thomas, please come forward!" he finished.

I couldn't believe it.

I stumbled up to the front, shook hands with Don, and took my certificate from Anita. All I could say was, "Thanks!" Then I turned to sit down, but I was stopped in my tracks by a burst of applause.

"All right, Kristy!" I heard Charlie yell.

Somehow I found my seat, and I sat through the rest of the ceremony with a huge grin on my face. I felt great! Not only had I learned something new, but I'd really learned it well. I was pretty proud of myself.

It was fun to watch my friends receive their certificates. When the ceremony was over, we went into the next room, where a reception with cookies and juice would take place.

"Congratulations, Kristy!" said Dawn. "I'm

so mad at myself. All I missed was one question on the written evaluation — and it was just a dumb mistake."

"Well, we all passed, and that's the main thing," I said. "Plus, it was a lot of fun, wasn't it?" I stood with my friends, laughing and talking about the course.

About five of the expectant mothers came up to us during the reception to congratulate me — and to ask for the club's phone number! Luckily, I'd thought ahead and made sure to bring some of our fliers, so I had something to give them.

Mrs. Salem brought Ricky and Rose over to say good-bye. "I may be calling you someday," she said to us. "These guys know how to wear out their mommy!"

"Sure," said Claudia. "We'd love to sit for you."

I excused myself from the group and joined Anita and Don. "Thanks for being such great teachers," I said. "You really made the course fun!"

Ethan poked his head out from behind Anita's skirt. "Will you baby-sit for me someday?" he asked me. I guess he'd gotten over his shyness.

"Sure, Ethan," I said. "Anytime." I smiled at Anita and Don and said good-bye.

* * *

My friends and I had decided to hold our own little celebration after the graduation ceremony, so, once the reception was over, we headed for Claud's room, our usual meeting spot.

Claud passed out some brownies she'd made (she had pretzels for Dawn and Stacey) and poured us each some diet soda. "Here's to the graduates!" she said, and we "clinked" our paper cups.

We talked some more about the class and the people in it. "Can you believe how huge Mrs. Nielsen got?" asked Stacey. "I can't imagine having a belly that big."

"I wonder if she'll really have the baby today," said Mary Anne. "How exciting."

Suddenly, in the midst of our celebration, I remembered that I'd promised to let Mrs. Prezzioso know right away when I had completed the infant-care course. I reached for the phone and called her.

"That's great, Kristy!" she said when I'd told her the news. "Can you start a week from Monday? I'll need you every Monday and Thursday from three until five, for four weeks all together."

"Sure," I said. "I'm looking forward to it."

"So is Jenny," said Mrs. Prezzioso. "And I'm sure if Andrea could talk, she'd say she was, too."

Just as I said good-bye and hung up, I heard Andrea squeal in the background, and I felt a little twinge of uneasiness. I was going to be taking care of a real baby soon.

Was I ready?

CHAPTER 6

When the time came for my first baby-sitting job with Jenny and Andrea, I did feel ready. I had gone over all my notes and reread every pamphlet and handout that Don and Anita had given us. I was sure that I was prepared for anything that might happen that day. After all, I had aced the course, right?

Well, partly right. That day, I found out that taking care of an infant is one thing, but that taking care of an infant *and* her four-year-old sister is quite another.

"Hi, Kristy, come on in!" said Mrs. Prezzioso when she answered the door that afternoon. She was speaking in a hushed tone, and I gave her a curious look. "Andrea's asleep," she said quietly. "She just went down for a short nap. She'll probably wake up in a half hour or so."

"KRISTY!!!" yelled Jenny, flying down the hall toward me.

51

I caught her and gave her a quick squeeze. "*Shhh*, Jenny. Let's not wake Andrea for a little while, okay?" I whispered.

"Okay," she whispered back. "Can we play Candy Land?"

Mrs. Prezzioso laughed. "I told you she was excited about this," she said. "She loves being a big sister — you'll see that when Andrea wakes up. But she also needs plenty of attention when the two of you are alone together."

I noticed that Jenny wasn't as dressed up as she usually is. I guess Mrs. P. doesn't have the time these days to create perfect outfits for every occasion. Jenny always used to look like a model in a clothing catalog. She'd be dressed in prim white dresses with yards of lace, matching socks, and hair ribbons. But lately she's been looking more like a regular little girl.

For that matter, Mrs. P. didn't look quite like she used to, either. Mary Anne always said that Mrs. P. looked like she had just stepped out of one of those magazines that have articles with titles like "A Dozen Glamorous New Ways to Use Leftover Meatloaf." But that day she simply appeared nice and neat, like any mother on her way to a meeting of her daughter's preschool board.

I guess having a four-year-old *and* a baby is keeping Mrs. P. pretty busy.

She began to run through some hurried instructions as she put on her jacket and searched for her car keys. "I've left some of Andrea's bottles in the refrigerator — they're all made up and all you have to do is put them in the bottle warmer when you need one," she said. "Her diapers are in the little closet beneath the changing table," she went on. "And if she — oh, dear, I'm late," she said, looking at her watch.

"Don't worry, Mommy," said Jenny. "I'll be a good helper. I know how to take care of Andrea."

"That's right, sweetie," said Mrs. P., bending to kiss Jenny. "You're a wonderful sister and a big help to your mommy and daddy. You be good for Kristy, all right?"

Jenny nodded and gave her mother a hug. "*Now* can we play Candy Land?" she asked, turning to me.

I laughed. "Sure, Jenny. 'Bye, Mrs. P. Have a good meeting."

As soon as the front door closed, Jenny grabbed my hand and pulled me into the living room. She pulled Candy Land off a shelf in a big cabinet.

"Let's bring it outside to play," she said. "I like to play Candy Land out in the front yard, under my favorite tree."

"Oh, Jenny," I said. "We can't. What if Andrea woke up and we didn't hear her?"

"But I *want* to play outside!" she said, looking stubborn. Now *that* sounded like the old, spoiled Jenny, the one who was used to always getting her way. I was going to have to be firm.

"Remember what your mommy said about being a good helper?" I asked. "I need you to help me listen for Andrea. And to do that, we'll have to play inside."

"Okay," said Jenny immediately. "I'll set up the game." She pulled out the box and opened it.

Just then, I heard a sound from upstairs. Was that Andrea?

"All ready!" said Jenny.

"*Shhh* . . . " I whispered. "Just a second. Did you hear that?" I heard the sound again, and this time I was sure. Andrea was waking up.

"Yea!" said Jenny. "Andrea's awake. Let's go play with her."

I headed upstairs to the nursery, with Jenny at my heels. I was surprised at how easily she'd given up her game of Candy Land. (I can't say I was all that sorry to have missed out on it, myself. Candy Land is *so* boring!) As we entered the room, I saw Andrea lying in her crib, on her stomach. She had pushed herself up with her arms and was holding her head up — a little unsteadily — and looking around as she gave her soft cries.

"Hi, Andrea!" I said softly. "Oh, she's so cute," I said to Jenny.

"I helped pick out her outfit for today," said Jenny proudly. "Pink is my favorite color, and it's hers, too." She walked over to the crib, stuck her hand between the railings, and patted her sister's foot. "Andrea-Bandrea," she said. "Hi-hi!"

I let Andrea study my face for a minute. She looked a little confused; no doubt she had expected her mother instead of me. But she didn't seem all that upset about it. I'm sure that having Jenny there helped. At least one person in the room was familiar to her.

When I figured I'd given her enough time to get used to my face, I bent down and lifted her out of the crib.

"Do you need a new diaper?" I asked her. She gurgled in reply. I checked to see if she was wet. "Looks like you're okay for now," I said. I was holding her carefully, just the way I'd been taught in class.

Suddenly, she started to cry, and I mean *really* cry. Her screams were so loud that I wanted to cover my ears. But I couldn't do that while I was holding her. Jenny could, though. And she did.

She stood with her hands over her ears,

shouting, "Make her stop! I hate it when she cries like that!" Jenny's eyes were squinched shut, and she looked like she was in pain.

What a racket.

I jiggled Andrea. I walked around the room with her. I spoke to her in a soothing, calm voice. She kept on screaming. And so did Jenny.

"Jenny," I said, raising my voice so I could be heard over both of them. "That's enough. I don't like the noise, either, but it doesn't help any when you yell also. Let's go downstairs and get Andrea a bottle, okay?"

She took her hands off her ears right away. "Okay!" she said. "I'll show you how to make it warm." She ran down the hall and I followed, carrying the still-wailing Andrea.

When we reached the kitchen, Jenny ran to the refrigerator and threw open the door. Wow! Mrs. P. had left enough bottles to last us a week. I guess she wanted to make sure that Andrea wouldn't go hungry, but it looked as if she'd gone overboard.

Jenny reached for one of the bottles — and knocked over a bowl of spaghetti that had been left unwrapped on a top shelf.

"Oh, *no*," I muttered. Andrea kept screaming. Jenny looked at me guiltily.

"I didn't mean — " she began.

"That's okay, Jenny." I said. "Tell you what.

Let's get the bottle into the warmer, and then you can help me clean up the mess."

Once I'd turned on the bottle warmer (I was really glad the Prezziosos had one, since warming a bottle in a pan on the stove — as we'd been taught in class — sounded a lot more complicated), I set to work cleaning up the mess in the refrigerator. It wasn't easy to do, with a crying baby in one arm. Jenny was "helping," but, although she was eager, she made the mess worse instead of better.

I stood up to rinse out a sponge and looked at the clock. Three-thirty. I'd only been there for half an hour! How was I going to last until five?

The bell on the bottle warmer went off just as I wiped up the last of the spaghetti. I sat down at the kitchen table, getting into a good "feeding" position. Andrea was still yelling, but as soon as I put the bottle into her mouth, her crying stopped.

What a relief.

Jenny sat down next to us and watched eagerly as Andrea sucked at the bottle. "See how her eyes open and close?" she said. "Look at her little hands."

Jenny was obviously in love with her baby sister.

Andrea ate and ate. My arm started to fall asleep, but I didn't want to bother her by shift-

57

ing my position. After awhile, Jenny started to squirm in her seat. She was becoming restless.

"Jenny," I said. "After Andrea finishes her bottle I'll strap her into her seat and she can watch while we make cookies."

"Yea!" shouted Jenny. Andrea "startled" at the noise. Anita had told us about that reflex. Babies do it when they hear a sudden sound. Her whole body seemed to jump, and her eyes flew wide open. For a minute I thought she was going to start crying again, but then she relaxed.

When she was finished with her bottle, I put her into her bouncer seat and strapped her in carefully. Then I set out the ingredients for cookies, and Jenny and I began our project.

We were soon interrupted when Andrea started to cry again. She was grabbing at her stomach, and I realized that she must have gas. I'd forgotten to burp her!

Then, just when she had settled down and I had turned back to measuring and sifting the flour, she began to cry once more. "What is it this time?" I asked.

"Diaper, probably," said Jenny. The voice of experience. And she was right.

I changed Andrea without a hitch.

But we never got to make the cookies. There was one interuption after another, all afternoon. Jenny was disappointed, but all I could do was apologize. It was just too hard to take care of Andrea's needs and do special projects like baking at the same time.

I realized that I had to take it easy. I didn't have to be Super-sitter. I just needed to be a responsible sitter. Next time I would know.

At the stroke of five, Mrs. P. rushed in. I hadn't had a chance to finish cleaning up the kitchen, so I started to apologize. "I'm sorry for the mess," I said. "We were — "

"That's okay," she interrupted. "Look at this! Doesn't this look like fun?" She showed me a piece of paper she was waving around. It was an entry form for the baby parade. "I got it at Jenny's school. She's too old to be in it, but I'm *dying* to enter Andrea. She'll need a costume and decorations for her stroller. . . . "

"It does look like fun," I said. "In fact, I was thinking of — "

But she didn't let me finish my sentence. "You'll help me, won't you, Kristy? I won't have time to do much, but I'll be glad to pay you extra if you could help."

"Oh — I — well . . . " I began. I had really wanted to enter Emily, and I didn't see how I could do both. "I'm not sure I'll have the time," I said finally.

"Okay, well why don't you think about it?"

she asked. "Let me know in a few days."

I agreed, and after she'd paid me I said good-bye to the girls and headed out the door. Mrs. P. sure was excited about the parade, I thought. She hadn't even remembered to ask me how the afternoon went!

CHAPTER 7

Wednesday

You know, ever since we took that cource on babys, I've notised that they can reely be a lot of fun. I used to think that they din't do much at all exsept cry and sleep. Well, in a way that's still true. But now I know some ways to play with them, and I know how to figgure out why they're crying... Did you guys ever notice how inkredibely cute Lucy Newton has goten lately?

Claud was sitting that day for a couple of our favorite kids, Jamie Newton (he's four) and his baby sister, Lucy. Jamie's always been a sweet little boy, and Lucy is just about the happiest baby I've ever known. She's always smiling and gurgling happily, even when she's just woken up.

"Hi, Claudia!" said Jamie, flinging open the door about two seconds after Claud had rung the bell. "I like your earrings!"

Claud, as usual, was wearing some pretty wild earrings that day. And, of course, they were coordinated with her outfit. Here's what she was wearing (I saw her later that day at our meeting): an oversized red blouse with black buttons, green leggings with white, tie-dyed streaks, and black high-top sneakers with all kinds of buckles and snaps on them. (The laces were untied, which I guess is the cool way to wear them. I'd be tripping over them all day, but Claud can pull it off.)

Can you guess what her earrings were? Dangling watermelon slices. Get it? She was dressed like a watermelon, head to toe. And, of course, Jamie loved the effect.

"I'm going to be a pumpkin for Halloween," he said. (Halloween's about three million months away, but you know how kids are.

They like to plan ahead for their favorite holidays.) "Maybe you can help me with my costume."

"Sure, Jamie," said Claudia. "I'd love to." Just then, Mrs. Newton came into the front hall. She was carrying Lucy, holding her car keys, and trying to put on her coat at the same time.

"Here," said Claudia. "I'll take her." Lucy clung to her mother for just a second, but when Claud made a funny face at her, she burst out laughing and fell into Claud's arms.

"Thanks, Claudia," said Mrs. Newton. "I'm just going to run a few errands, but I'll be sure to be back by five-fifteen so you can make your meeting."

"I may take them to the library, if that's all right," said Claudia. She'd been thinking that it would be fun to take Jamie to the children's room and show him the new puppet theater. She'd heard about it from her mom, who's the head librarian.

"Liberry! Liberry!" chanted Jamie immediately. "We're going to the liberry!" He jumped up and down.

"That sounds great," said Mrs. Newton. "Lucy's stroller is on the porch. Oh, and there's a pile of books you could return for me. They're on top of Jamie's dresser.

Thanks!" She grabbed her pocketbook, gave Jamie and Lucy each a quick kiss, and rushed out the door.

"Let's go, Claudia!" said Jamie, pulling at her hand. "Let's go to the liberry!"

"I'm glad you want to go," said Claudia, "but first we need to make sure Lucy's wearing a clean diaper, and pack a bag with a bottle in it, in case she needs a snack while we're there."

"*I* need a snack, right now!" said Jamie. "I'm hungry. But after that, can we go?"

"Sure," said Claud, and for the next fifteen minutes she was very busy trying to get Lucy ready for their short trip, making a peanut butter and honey sandwich (on toast) for Jamie, and rounding up the library books, which Jamie had *un*stacked from the pile on his dresser.

Then it took another fifteen minutes to dress Jamie and Lucy for the outdoors. Jamie "helped" by shoving Lucy's feet into her zip-up suit and then jamming the zipper as he tried to close it. Luckily for Claud, Lucy just smiled and babbled happily, and her dark blue eyes sparkled as she looked into Claud's brown ones.

Claud had a good time pushing Lucy's stroller down the street. Lucy was so cute that everyone who saw her stopped to smile. Some people bent down and asked Lucy questions in baby-talk.

Jamie walked beside the stroller, proud of his little sister and of the attention she was getting. He told anyone who asked how old she was. He never forgot to add his own age, too, Claud noticed, as well as his birthday.

"Maybe I'll get a lot of presents if all those people know my birthday," he explained happily.

When Claud entered the children's room at the library, the noise almost knocked her over. The room was *packed* with screaming, yelling, jumping kids. She grabbed Jamie's hand and held Lucy closer. (She'd left the stroller at the entrance and was carrying Lucy.)

"What's going on?" she yelled over the clamor, when she'd caught the eye of the children's librarian.

"We just had an after-school program," the woman yelled back. "And it's almost time for story hour. It should empty out pretty soon."

She was right. Claud took her charges over to a corner to read a book to them and wait out the crowds. After a few minutes the room had grown much quieter. Then she showed Jamie the puppet theater. He loved it, and started putting on a show about Little Red Riding Hood. Claudia and Lucy watched.

"Now I'm going to get you," Jamie said in

as deep a voice as he could manage, waving the wolf puppet menacingly. "Oh, no!" he answered in a high, squeaky voice. He danced the girl puppet backward. Lucy waved her hands and shrieked with laughter.

The show went on until Little Red Riding Hood had been saved by various characters, including Spiderman. Finally, Claud realized they'd better go home if she wanted to get to the club meeting on time.

"Order!" I said, as the clock on Claud's desk turned to 5:30. All of us were there, sprawled out around the room. Dawn had been showing us a postcard her brother had sent her from Venice Beach, California. On the front was a photo of a roller-skater wearing an outrageous outfit.

"That picture reminds me," I said, after we'd finished discussing club business — and after we'd answered a few job calls. "What kind of costume do you think I could make Emily for the baby parade?"

"I thought you were supposed to be thinking about *Andrea's* costume," said Mary Anne. I'd told my friends about how Mrs. P. had asked me to help her.

"Oh, I know," I answered. "I just can't decide what to do about the baby parade. I'm not even sure if my mom will let me enter

Emily, but I'm dying to. On the other hand, if I don't help Mrs. P. with Andrea, she might not even want me to finish out the next three weeks of baby-sitting that she hired me for."

"She wouldn't fire you just for that!" said Stacey.

"I sure hope not," I answered.

"You know," said Claudia. "Lucy Newton ought to be entered in the parade. She is the cutest thing in the universe."

"She is cute," said Jessi. "So's Squirt, for that matter. I bet he could win a prize."

"What about Laura and Gabbie Perkins?" asked Mary Anne. "They'd love to be in the parade, I bet."

"So would Eleanor Marshall," added Dawn. "I sat for her the other day, and she is a total doll. She is so, so cute."

I felt it coming. An idea. One of the best ideas I'd had yet. "I know," I said suddenly. "How about if we get a whole bunch of babies together and enter them as a group in the Float Division?" I was excited. "I could help you guys with that, *and* also get Andrea ready for the Stroller Division. That way, we can all enter whatever babies we want! It'll be fun making the float, won't it?" I had gotten so carried away that I was already assuming we'd do it.

"You know," said Stacey, "I think that's a great idea!"

Everybody else agreed with her, so we spent the rest of the meeting calling all the parents we could think of to ask their permission for our plan. Of course, Mrs. P. was the first parent I called, and she was thrilled that I'd be helping her with Andrea's costume. This was going to be the best baby parade Stoneybrook had ever seen!

CHAPTER 8

"So are you guys all ready to hear my great idea for our float?" I asked. I couldn't wait to tell them my plan. I knew they'd love it. It was Saturday morning, and we were all lounging around in the living room at Dawn and Mary Anne's house. We'd decided to have our baby parade planning meeting there, where we could spread out and talk all morning with no interruptions. (Mary Anne's dad was working in the yard, and Dawn's mom had gone off to do some errands.)

I looked around the room at my friends. Nobody had begged me to tell them my idea, but then again, none of them had said I shouldn't. "Okay, here's what we'll do. The theme will be — get this — Take Me Out to the Ball Game!" I scanned their faces to see their reactions to my idea, but I couldn't tell what they thought. "We'll dress the babies in little baseball uniforms and decorate the float

like a baseball diamond. It'll be so, so cute!"
I went on.

"You've got to be kidding," said Dawn in a
flat voice. "That has to be the worst idea I've
ever heard. Babies playing baseball?"

I was crushed. But I didn't have time to
defend my idea because Dawn kept on talking.

"*I* think we should do something really different, something nobody else in Stoneybrook
would ever think about. Like Surfin' USA!"
She smiled at all of us. "We'll dress the babies
in really cool-looking outfits, put them on surf-
boards, and decorate the float to look like the
ocean."

I rolled my eyes. Why were surfing babies
any better than babies playing baseball? I
heard Mary Anne giggle. Dawn glared at her.

"I'm sorry," Mary Anne said. "It's just that
the idea of baby surfers seems kind of silly to
me. I thought we'd do something that was
more related to kids, like maybe acting out a
nursery rhyme."

"Oh?" asked Dawn. I could tell she was a
little hurt that Mary Anne had made fun of
her idea. Well, now she knew how it felt.
"What nursery rhyme did you have in mind,
Mary Anne?"

"Three Little Kittens," answered Mary Anne
proudly. "We'd dress up the babies like kittens, and I could knit little mittens for them

. . . And of course, Tigger could be on the float, too."

"I get it," said Stacey. "You came up with that idea just so you could work out a way for your kitten to be on the float. That's ridiculous! This is a baby parade, not a pet show."

Mary Anne hung her head and sniffled. She cries so easily.

"I'm sorry, Mary Anne," said Stacey. "But don't you think that idea is a little childish? I think the judges would be more impressed with something a little more sophisticated."

Mary Anne wiped her eyes with the back of her hand. "Okay, let's hear it," she said.

"What?" asked Stacey.

"Your idea for our float," answered Mary Anne. "Obviously you think you have a great one. Let's hear it."

"Well," said Stacey. She closed her eyes for a moment and then started talking very fast, as if she were nervous that someone would interrupt her. "I was thinking that we could do a float called 'New York, New York.' It could be a model of the skyline. You know, the Empire State Building and all that? And we could dress up the babies in tuxedos and evening gowns."

I held back a giggle. "Very glamorous," I said, trying to look serious.

Claudia didn't bother to hold back *her* giggles. She burst out laughing. "Stacey, I don't believe it. You've gone off your rocker. Babies in tuxedos? We'd be the biggest joke in the parade."

Stacey crossed her arms and sat silently, frowning at the floor.

I looked around the room.

"How about you, Mal?" I asked. Apparently, we'd all come with ideas, so I figured I might as well let everybody have a chance to speak.

"Oh, well I —" she broke off in midsentence, looking as if she'd like to disappear.

"What, Mal?" asked Jessi. "Come on, you can tell us."

"I was thinking of doing *Misty of Chincoteague*," she said in one breath.

"WHAT?" we all said at once.

"*Misty,*" she said. "My favorite book. I thought we could act it out."

"What," said Jessi. "Dress the babies like wild ponies?" She raised her eyebrows. I heard a few giggles exploding around the room.

"I don't know," said Mallory, sounding miserable. "I hadn't really thought it out, I guess."

The giggles got louder, and soon we were all laughing so hard we could barely breathe. Every time the laughing began to die down, someone would say, "Ponies!" or "Surfers!", and it would start all over again. My stomach hurt, and tears were rolling down my face.

Finally, we managed to get ourselves under control. "Claudia," I said, once I had found my voice. "What about you? We never heard *your* idea."

She blushed. "I know," she said. "And now you're never going to. It was just as dumb as all the others."

"Come on!" said Stacey. "You've got to tell. *We* all made fools of ourselves. Why should you be the only one who didn't?"

We pestered her until she broke down. "Oh, all right," she said. "It was an idea about babies from outer space — you know, like something you'd see in those supermarket newspapers: 'Woman gives birth to baby from Mars.' "

We were too stunned even to laugh. That had to be the worst idea of all!

"I know, I know," said Claud. "That's why I didn't want to tell you guys. But listen, I think Mary Anne is on to something. I think acting out a nursery rhyme is a great idea, even if that kitten one isn't the best choice."

I looked around the room. Everybody was nodding. "You know," I said. "I think Claud's right. So what nursery rhyme could we do?"

"We need one with lots of characters," said

Dawn. "I mean, we've already got five babies, right?"

"Let's see," I said, checking the list we'd made. "Squirt and Emily, Lucy Newton, Eleanor Marshall, and Laura Perkins. That's five. I guess Gabbie didn't want to be in the parade."

"Okay, let's think," said Stacey. The room was quiet for a few minutes.

"All I can think of are rhymes with two characters!" said Mallory. "Like Jack and Jill, or Peter Peter Pumpkin Eater."

"I know," said Dawn. "This isn't as easy as you'd think."

Then somebody called out the idea that we ended up agreeing on. I can't even remember who it was, and neither can anyone else. I don't think anybody wants to take responsibility for it, even though we all thought it was a great idea. At the time.

The Old Woman Who Lived in a Shoe. That was our idea. It sounded like a lot of fun.

"We'll need more that five babies for that one," said Mary Anne.

"But we don't know too many other kids under three," I answered. "Where can we get more babies?" Then I thought of the infant-care course we'd taken. We'd met a lot of babies there! At least some of those new parents would have to be interested in entering their kids in the baby parade.

"Great idea," said Mary Anne, when I'd blurted out what I'd been thinking. "And I even have some of their phone numbers in the record book. We can call them right away."

Good old Mary Anne. What an efficient club secretary. We made some phone calls then and there, and before we knew it we had four more babies lined up.

"You will be on the float with them, won't you?" asked Mrs. Salem, when I called to see if Ricky and Rose could be involved.

"Of course," I answered. And I said the same thing to the last mother we called, who asked the same question. But, of course, we hadn't really figured out how *we* were going to dress — or how we were going to handle nine babies, for that matter.

"Nine babies is definitely more than enough," said Stacey. "I don't see how we could handle any more than that. And as for what we should wear — one of us can dress up like the Old Woman, and the others can dress like her older children. That way, we'll all fit into the theme."

We agreed, although we didn't stop to decide which of us would be the Old Woman. We'd made enough decisions for the day.

"We can build the float in my backyard, so we can be near all my art supplies," said Claudia. "I hope you realize that it's not going to be easy to build a giant float, though."

"Oh, we'll figure it out," I said. "I'll ask Charlie if he can help us. I was thinking that he could pull the float behind the Junk Bucket." (That's Charlie's old car.) I knew he'd be glad to help. He's usually pretty good about things like that.

"So we're all set, right?" asked Stacey. "I have to meet my mom now so we can go to the mall."

"All set," I said.

That showed how much I knew.

CHAPTER 9

On Monday afternoon when I went to the Prezziosos' to sit, Jenny flung the door open before I'd even rung the bell. She must have been waiting for me. "Guess what!" she said. "Mommy figured out what Andrea's costume should be."

"That's great." I said. "I can't wait to hear about it." I thought she'd tell me about the costume, but instead she heaved a big sigh.

"I wish *I* could be in the parade," she said, "and wear a pretty costume and everything."

"I know," I said. "But you're a big girl, and the parade's just for babies."

She nodded. "Sometimes I wish I wasn't such a big girl," she said wistfully."Sometimes I wish I was still a baby."

I felt bad for her. She must have been feeling kind of left out. "But remember," I said. "Big girls get to do all kinds of things that babies can't do, like helping to bake cookies, and — "

Just then, Mrs. Prezzioso burst into the front hall. "Oh!" she said. "You're here, Kristy. I didn't hear the doorbell."

"I know," I said. "Jenny — "

But she cut me off. "Did you hear about Andrea's costume?" she asked. "I think it's going to be absolutely precious." She seemed really excited.

"I heard that you chose a theme," I answered, "but Jenny hasn't told me what it is."

"Oh, I know you're going to love it, Kristy," she said, smiling happily. "I've decided to dress her as Queen Andrea!"

Queen Andrea?

I gulped. "That — that sounds wonderful!" I said, trying to seem enthusiastic. It seemed like a pretty weird idea to me, if you want to know the truth.

"And she's going to have a crown, and a long, long dress!" added Jenny.

"That's right," said Mrs. P. "Let me show you what I've found so far." She threw open the door to the hall closet. "Here's her crown," she said, showing me a gold crown (made of plastic) with fake jewels all over it. "And she's going to wear this big wig, like they wore in the old days." She showed me something that looked like my neighbor's cat.

I didn't know what to say.

"Oh! I'll be late if I don't get going," said Mrs. P. suddenly, looking at her watch. "Andrea's asleep, but she should be ready to wake up soon."

I trailed her out the door. She had planned Andrea's costume without my help. I wondered if she still wanted me to work on it. "Is there anything else I should do about getting Andrea ready for the parade?" I asked. I was hoping that she'd changed her mind and didn't need my help after all.

"Oh, that's right!" she said. "I almost forgot. I want you to figure out how to make her stroller look like a coach."

A coach. Oh, sure.

"You can use any materials you find in my sewing room," she said. "I'm going to be pushing her in the parade," she added. "And I want her to look fabulous so she'll make a good impression on the judges. I would really, really like her to win first prize in her division. Wouldn't that be fantastic?"

"Fantastic," I echoed. I waved at Mrs. P. as she jumped into her car. Wow! She was getting carried away with this parade stuff. And she sure sounded as if she wanted Andrea to win a prize. I suddenly felt like I was under a lot of pressure.

What if Andrea *didn't* win? Would Mrs. P.

decide that I was a terrible sitter because I hadn't been able to make the stroller into a perfect coach? Would she fire me? What would that do to the reputation of the club?

Just then, I heard Andrea's cries from upstairs. She was ready to get up. "C'mon, Jenny," I said, trying to put my worries aside. "Let's go get Queen Andrea."

It turned out that Her Royal Highness had a wet diaper, so the first order of business was to get her into a dry one. Then Jenny decided she was hungry, so we trooped downstairs for a snack. Just as I was cleaning up from that, Andrea started to wail, and I realized that she must have been hungry, too.

I got her a bottle and we sat on the couch while she drank. Jenny jumped around the room, waving her arms and tunelessly singing the theme from *Sesame Street*. "Watch me!" she said, and she bent down to do a somersault.

It was a pretty crooked one, but she stood up proudly afterward and looked my way. "Very good, Jenny!" I said.

"Look what else I can do," she said, as she took off into a cartwheel. *Bam!* She careened into the couch.

"Oh, Jenny," I said. "Are you all right?"

"I'm fine," she said brightly. "Don't you think I'm a good cartwheeler? I could do gymtastics in the parade!"

"That's gym*n*astics," I said. "And yes, you're a good cartwheeler. But cartwheels are for outdoors, not for the living room. And as for the parade, remember what I told you? It's just for babies."

Jenny pouted for a minute or two but brightened when she saw that her baby sister had finished her bottle. "Let's put Andrea's costume on her," she said. "Wait till you see how it looks."

She led me to the closet, and we got out the parts of the costume that Mrs. P. had stored there. Besides the crown and the wig, Jenny pulled out a long cloak with fake fur trim, and a big lacy ruff for Andrea to wear around her neck.

We sat Andrea on the living room floor and dressed her up. Boy, did she look funny! The wig slipped down over one eye, and the crown sat crookedly on top. The cloak was so long that she'd have tripped over it — if she knew how to walk. And the ruff? Well, her chin — and half her face — kind of disappeared into it, so that you couldn't see how cute she was anymore.

Jenny giggled. "She looks silly," she said.

I agreed, but I thought it might be better if I didn't say so out loud. "I think she looks very nice," I said (lying through my teeth).

Andrea smiled at me, and then, all of a sudden, she gave a little burp.

"Oh, no!" I said. Andrea had spit up all over the ruff. It was my fault, too. I'd forgotten to burp her after her bottle. I hurried Andrea out of the Queen outfit and cleaned the ruff as well as I could.

Then I decided that I'd better start thinking about how to make that stroller into a coach. "Come on, Jenny," I said. "You can help me figure this out." I took Andrea into the sewing room and set her on the floor in her infant seat. That way, I could keep an eye on her while I worked. I gave her some plastic rings and rattles to keep her busy. Then I looked around the room to see what kind of materials Mrs. P. had left for me.

"*Somewhere, over the rainbow —* " sang Jenny in a piercing voice. She stood in the middle of the room, with her hands clasped in front of her, just like Dorothy in *The Wizard of Oz.*

"Jenny," I said. She was not only loud, she was totally off-key.

"*We're off to see the Wizard,*" she sang, even louder.

"JENNY!" I said.

She stopped short. "What?" she asked. "I'm just showing you what a good singer I am. Maybe I could sing in the parade."

"Jenny, you can't do gymnastics in the parade, and you can't sing in the parade. You can *watch* the parade, but you can't be in it. You're too old!"

Jenny bit her lower lip and stared at the floor. I gave her a quick hug and said, "Let's see what we can do to decorate Andrea's stroller, okay?"

Jenny nodded sadly. "Okay," she said.

I pulled out some bolts of material from the closet. There was this stuff with gold sequins all over it, and some other fabric with silver threads running through it. "We could make a canopy out of these," I said. I set them on the floor by Andrea's seat — and noticed she'd thrown down every one of the toys I'd given her. "Oh, Andrea," I said, laughing.

"She doesn't do it on purpose," said Jenny. "Mommy says that she's just not old enough to hold onto things for very long."

"I know," I said. "I'm not mad." I piled all the toys back into Andrea's lap. "There you go, Your Highness," I said.

Andrea smiled at me and said, "Blurg."

"Okay," I said. "So we'll have a gold-and-silver canopy. What else?"

But Jenny didn't answer. She was too busy twirling around the room, her hands in ballerina positions. Every so often she'd stop and do some tap-dance steps, and then go back to her *pirouettes*.

"What are you doing now?" I asked, although I had a fairly good idea.

"Dancing!" she answered breathlessly. "Maybe I can *dance* in the parade."

I rolled my eyes. She just wasn't getting the message. "Jenny," I said, feeling like I'd already explained it fifty times. "The parade is just for babies. Now be a big girl and help me decorate Andrea's stroller. We can have fun doing it, and then when you watch the parade and see Andrea win a prize, you'll know that you helped." That was dangerous. I was practically promising her that Andrea would win a prize. But I was desperate.

Jenny brightened. "Then it will kind of be *my* prize, too?"

"That's right," I said.

"Okay."

Jenny and I spent the rest of the afternoon creating the most ridiculous-looking "coach" you can imagine. But when Mrs. P. came home, she *loved* it!

CHAPTER 10

Tuesday

I love babies, and not just my little brother Squirt, either. I love all babies — their little toes, their soft skin, their goofy smiles. I love to tickle them and make them laugh. I love to give them their bottles and watch them fall asleep in my lap. I even love to change their diapers — because it makes them so happy to be clean and dry. But today, for the first time, I began to wonder if there

might be such a
thing as too many
babies!

I think I understand what made Jessi write that in the club notebook. We ended up having kind of a baby convention that afternoon, and it *was* a little bit overwhelming.

Jessi was sitting for Becca and Squirt that day, because her parents were both at work and her Aunt Cecelia had gone out to do some shopping. Her first half hour was fine. Squirt was totally captivated by *Sesame Street*. His favorite character is this little guy Elmo, who isn't on very often, so Squirt has to watch carefully in order to catch him.

Meanwhile, Jessi was showing Becca, for the six-hundredth time, the five positions for ballet. Becca was doing all right at first, second, and third positions, but every time she tried fourth she would get twisted up and fall over.

Becca does not have the same natural grace as Jessi.

But she didn't let it bother her. In fact, every time Becca fell down she would squeal, then she'd giggle, shrug, and get up to try again. Finally, though, she grew tired of the game.

"Let's do something else," she said to Jessi.

Jessi looked at Squirt. He was singing along with the *Sesame Street* song, which meant that the show was ending. "Okay," she said. "How about if we go over to Claudia's? I think they're starting to build the float over there today."

"Yea!" said Becca. Jessi had told her about the baby parade and about the float that Squirt was going to ride on. Becca was excited about the idea. "Maybe I can help to build it," she said.

Of course, Squirt didn't understand at all about the float, but he loves to take walks, so Jessi had no trouble convincing him to go over to Claudia's. He led the way to his stroller, climbed into it, and waited impatiently for Jessi to start pushing.

"Go!" he said, grinning. "Go, GO!" He was hanging on tightly to his favorite toy of the moment, a red plastic fish.

Jessi let Becca push Squirt most of the way. Becca thinks that's the biggest treat. When they reached Claudia's backyard, Jessi saw that Claudia, Stacey, and Mallory were there already, working on the float.

Jessi was a little surprised, she told me later, at the *way* they were working. It was completely quiet in that yard. Nobody was laughing or talking.

"Hey, guys!" Jessi called. "How's it going?" Nobody gave her much of an answer. Each of them was too busy with the job she was doing. Jessi lifted Squirt out of his stroller and, carrying him, walked around to take a look at their projects.

Claudia was bending chicken wire into the shape of a humongous shoe. Jessi said later that she couldn't figure out exactly how and where the babies were supposed to fit into the plan. She offered Claud a suggestion, and Claud thanked her and kept on working.

Stacey was mixing paints, for whenever the float would be ready to decorate. She was trying out little dabs of color on a big sheet of cardboard. Jessi wondered whether she was mixing up *enough* paint — the shoe that Claudia was building looked so big. But all she said was, "I love that orangey-red color." Stacey looked up and smiled. She had a spot of yellow paint on her nose.

Mallory was sketching costumes for the babies. Jessi leaned over her shoulder. "Those are adorable," she said. "And they look like they'll be easy to make."

"That was my plan," said Mallory, pushing up her glasses with one finger. "And look at this great material I got. It was really cheap, but isn't it nice?" She held out a big bag to Jessi, who peeked into it.

"Nice," Jessi said. "Really nice." The material was a bright pink, and Jessi shuddered at the thought of how those costumes were going to look next to the orangey-red that Stacey had perfected. Talk about clashing!

But she didn't say a thing. Everybody was working so hard. Who was she to criticize them? If only they would *talk* to each other, she thought. But each seemed to have her own opinion on what the float should look like, and none of them appeared interested in what the others thought.

Since Becca was having a good time running around Claudia's backyard, Jessi decided she would hang around for awhile. She offered to help Mallory with her costume design, but Mallory shook her head.

"I've got it under control, Jessi," she said. "Thanks, though."

So Jessi and Squirt just sat and watched.

"Hey, what's up?" called Dawn, walking into the yard. Jamie and Lucy Newton were with her. She walked around just as Jessi had, checking on her friends' progress. "Looking good!" she said to Claud. "Nice work, Stace!" she said, looking at the paints. "I love those costumes," she remarked to Mallory. "They'll be terrific."

Dawn joined Jessi underneath a nearby tree. She was carrying Lucy, and Jamie had run off to play with Becca. "Oh, no!" she whispered, leaning close to Jessi. "Do those guys know what they're doing?"

Jessi giggled. *"Shhh!"* she said. "They're all working so hard — "

"I know," said Dawn. "Anyway, I'm sure it'll be a great float, no matter what."

Squirt and Lucy grinned at each other. Squirt waved hello with his red fish.

"Look!" said Jessi. "They like each other. I just realized that this is a great time for them to meet — *before* they're on the float together."

"You're right," said Dawn. She giggled. "Ms. Lucy Jane Newton, I'd like you to meet Mr. John Philip Ramsey Jr.," she said, holding her nose so that she sounded like a proper lady.

Jessi laughed. *"So* pleased to make your acquaintance," she said, holding her own nose and speaking for Squirt.

"Charmed, I'm sure," said Dawn.

"What *are* you guys up to?" asked Mary Anne. She had just entered the yard, carrying Laura Perkins. Gabbie and Myriah were following close behind her.

Dawn laughed and explained that they were making sure that Squirt and Lucy had been "properly introduced."

"Oh, in that case," said Mary Anne, "may I present Miss Laura Elizabeth Perkins?" Laura held out her hand to Lucy, as if she wanted to shake. Jessi, Dawn, and Mary Anne giggled.

That was when I arrived, with Jenny and Andrea. Jenny ran off to play with the other little kids, who were by then having a great time running around together. I sat down under the tree and "introduced" Andrea to the others. There we were, with all those babies. It was kind of awesome.

I hadn't gotten a good look at what Claudia, Mallory, and Stacey were doing, so Jessi and Dawn filled me in. I thought that maybe I should talk to them, but Mary Anne convinced me not to.

"Let them go on working," she said. "The float may look confusing, but I'm sure it'll come together soon."

"Besides," said Dawn. "We've got to watch these babies."

"Aren't they adorable?" said Jessi with a sigh, gazing at Squirt and Lucy. They were sitting next to each other, not actually "playing," but still getting along well.

"I just love babies," said Dawn. "This parade is going to be a blast!"

Just then, Lucy grabbed Squirt's fish. She had been eyeing it for several moments, and the temptation must have been too strong to resist any longer.

Squirt let out an earsplitting wail.

Lucy smiled and put the fish's tail in her mouth.

"Lucy, honey," said Dawn. "Give Squirt his fish."

Lucy ignored her.

Squirt cried louder.

Then Laura started to cry.

"What is it?" asked Mary Anne. "What's the matter, Laura?" She picked her up and held her close, jiggling her slightly to calm her.

Dawn finally got the fish away from Lucy and gave it back to Squirt. His cries started to die down, but Lucy's grew louder. To distract her, Dawn held her up to look at Andrea, who was sitting in my lap.

"See Andrea?" asked Dawn. "She's going to be in the parade, just like you. Only she won't be on the float. She's going to be in her very own stroller." Of course, Lucy didn't understand a thing Dawn was saying, but the distraction seemed to work and her crying finally stopped.

Laura was still crying, however, so Mary Anne decided to check her diaper.

Meanwhile, Andrea was becoming restless, so I decided to try Dawn's "distraction" technique. "That's Lucy," I said, holding Andrea up to see her. "She's going to be riding on a big, big float." Andrea gave Lucy a toothless grin.

Then she spit up, all over Lucy.

At the same time, Squirt dropped his fish, couldn't reach it, and started to cry again.

Laura was still wailing.

Claudia looked up from her chicken-wire sculpture. "Can't you guys keep those babies quiet?" she asked. "We're trying to get some work done here."

I almost blew up at her, but Mary Anne caught my eye and shook her head. She was right, I knew it. We didn't have time for a big fight, not if we wanted to get that float into the parade.

Somehow, we managed to clean up the babies and calm them down — and even enjoy the rest of the afternoon. But, as Jessi said in the notebook, the scene in Claudia's yard did make us wonder if there could be such a thing as too many babies.

CHAPTER 11

Thursday

I suppose you all think I should be apologizing for my behavior in Claud's yard today, but to tell you the truth, I don't think I should have to. I was only being honest. Besides, as the Marshalls' sitter, I think I owe it to them to make sure that Eleanor looks as good as possible on the float. I can't believe the parade is only two days away...

Maybe Dawn really did think she was being honest, but still, she *did* owe us an apology. Or at least she should have apologized to Mallory. But I'm getting ahead of myself here. Let me tell the story as it happened.

Dawn was sitting for Nina and Eleanor Marshall. We used to sit for them more often when the club first started, but then the Marshalls got a full-time housekeeper. Lately the Marshalls have been calling us again, since they cut back on the housekeeper's hours.

Nina is four, and she's a lot of fun. She's at that stage in which she's learning how to have real conversations with people, and some of the discussions she gets into are pretty funny.

Dawn said that Nina once told her about this friend of hers at her preschool. His name, said Nina, was Jimmytony. He was her "boyfriend," and he called her up all the time. Dawn thought that Jimmytony sounded like a great friend.

Later, Dawn found out that Jimmytony *was* a great friend — a great *imaginary* friend. Mrs. Marshall explained it to her one day. Nina had made him up, all on her own.

Eleanor is two, and she's incredibly cute. She's got blonde, wavy hair with a big cowlick in the front and gigantic blue eyes. She's just beginning to string words into sentences —

sort of. For example, if she and Nina are playing with Nina's Barbie, dressing her up for a night on the town, Eleanor will say "Barbie — dress — dancing!"

Eleanor likes to copy her big sister, and she tries to say and do everything Nina says and does, which isn't always easy for her.

Anyway, Dawn was sitting for the Marshall girls that Thursday afternoon. She'd told Mrs. Marshall about the float we were making for the parade (of course, she'd already gotten permission for Eleanor to be part of it), and Mrs. Marshall was excited.

"It's too bad Nina is too old to be on the float," said Mrs. Marshall, on her way out the door that day.

Dawn nodded. "I know," she said. "There are other kids we sit for who would like to be in the parade, too. But it'll be fun for Nina to watch her sister go by on our float. Right, Nina?"

Nina nodded. "Can we play hide-and-seek?" she asked, changing the subject.

Her mother laughed. "Well, I guess *she* doesn't mind that she's not going to be on the float! I'll leave you to your game."

As soon as she was out the door, Dawn found herself with Nina pulling her by one hand and Eleanor holding on to the other.

"Hide-and-seek!" yelled Nina.

"Hide! Seek!" yelled Eleanor.

Dawn had never played hide-and-seek with the girls, so she figured that they must have just learned the game and wanted to "teach" it to her. "Okay," she said. "What do we do first?"

"You close your eyes and count to ten while we hide," said Nina.

"Find!" said Eleanor.

"Right," said Nina. "Then you say 'Ready or not, here I come!' and you find us."

"Sounds like fun," said Dawn. "Let's play just in this room, though, okay?" They were in the living room, and she thought it might be a good idea to keep the game small. She didn't want to hunt all over the house for the girls.

As it turned out, she was worried for nothing.

The Marshall girls had their own version of hide-and-seek. Here's how it went: As soon as Dawn finished counting and said "Ready or not, here I come," both girls started to giggle in their hiding places. They weren't very well hidden, either. Nina was standing behind a lamp that was much smaller than she was, and Eleanor was simply facing into a corner of the room, figuring (Dawn thought) that if she couldn't see Dawn, Dawn couldn't see *her*.

Anyway Dawn began to prowl around the

room, thinking out loud about how to find the girls. "Now, where could they be?" she asked herself. "Where are those girls hiding?" The giggles grew louder and then turned into shrieks as the girls, unable to stand the suspense, ran out of their hiding places and flung themselves at Dawn.

"I found you!" Dawn cried, laughing. They played the game five more times, and each time the girls hid in exactly the same spots and Dawn found them just as quickly. It wasn't hide-and-seek the way Dawn had learned it, but Eleanor and Nina were having a great time anyway.

When they'd finished playing, Dawn suggested they go over to Claudia's to see how the float was coming along. "It should be almost done by now," she said.

But when they reached Claudia's backyard, Dawn took one look around and wanted to run back to the Marshalls'.

The float stood in the middle of the yard, looking like a lumpy, streaky red mountain. Claud is a talented artist, but I'd had the feeling that something as big as a float wasn't going to be as easy to make as we'd thought. Especially since she'd been trying to take all of our suggestions into account. She must have felt confused.

Claudia and Stacey were hovering around the float adding final touches. "Why didn't you mix more paint?" Claudia asked Stacey, as Dawn walked up to them. "This wasn't nearly enough. No wonder the float looks awful."

"I really don't think that the paint is the problem, Claudia," said Stacey. "I mean, look at the shape of this thing. Who would ever guess it was a shoe?" She turned to Dawn. "What would *you* think it was?" she asked.

"I — I don't know," said Dawn. She didn't want to get in the middle of their argument. "It looks fine," she said. "But — where do the babies sit?"

"Don't worry," I said. I had just arrived with Emily. "I have some ideas about that."

"Oh, you do, do you?" asked Claudia, her hands on her hips. "I'm the one who built the float. I've tried to use everyone's ideas, but that's only made it worse. So now I'm just going to do it my way."

"Okay, what's *your* way?" I asked.

"Well — " she said. It was obvious — to me, anyway — that she hadn't even thought about it.

I looked around. By then, Jessi had arrived with Squirt, and Mary Anne was just coming into the yard carrying Laura Perkins. I knew that Mallory was sitting for Jamie and Lucy Newton that day, and that they would probably be coming over, too.

"I know," I said. "How about a dress rehearsal? We can put the costumes on the babies who show up today and see how the kids look on the float."

Everybody agreed, so I ran up to Claud's room to use her phone. I called Mal at the Newtons'. "Can you bring the costumes over here?" I asked her.

"Sure," she said. "They're not quite finished, but we'll get an idea of how they look."

When she walked into Claud's yard, Mallory was carrying Lucy in one arm and a big brown bag in the other. "Here they are!" she said. She put the bag down and pulled out one of the costumes. The color was even brighter than I had remembered.

I took one for Emily, and Dawn grabbed one for Eleanor. Jessi got Squirt's, and Mary Anne found one that looked like it would fit Laura. Mal started to button Lucy into her costume.

The costumes looked (to me) like little clown suits, with ruffles down the front. I'm not sure what Mallory had in mind when she designed them, but they did look kind of cute once we'd gotten the babies into them.

I lifted Emily onto the float. Dawn set Eleanor down next to her. Right away, we both noticed how badly the costumes clashed with the color of the float, but neither of us said anything. We just looked at each other and raised our eyebrows.

Stacey, however, spoke up. "Good going, Mal," she said sarcastically. "Didn't you see what color the paint was going to be?"

Mallory blushed. "I — I thought this material would be good," she said. "It was on sale. Besides, *you* didn't ask *me* about *my* plans!"

"Let's not fight about it," I said. "So the costumes clash. Big deal. But Mallory, where are *our* costumes?"

Mal looked at me blankly.

"We're going to be on the float, too, you know," I said. "What are we going to wear?"

She put her hand over her mouth. "I didn't think of that," she said. "But there's no way I can make seven more costumes in two days. I haven't even finished these! Everyone's just going to have to make their own."

"Sheesh," I said. "As if *we've* got time."

"Oh, we can whip something together," said Stacey. "What's the big deal, anyway? We're going to look dumb no matter what we're wearing, since we'll all be riding on this lumpy old float that doesn't look anything like a shoe."

Claudia jumped to her feet. "Now, wait a

minute," she said. "It would have looked more like a shoe if I could have made it *my* way instead of listening to all of you guys and your bright ideas!"

At that moment, Eleanor started wailing. After about two seconds, Squirt joined her. Soon all the babies were crying.

Dawn shook her head. "I bet they're crying because their costumes look so stupid," she whispered to Mary Anne.

But Mallory heard her. "Stupid?" she repeated. "I'd like to see you do better!" She burst into tears. Jessi tried to comfort her, but Mal pushed her away. "You probably think they look dumb, too," she said.

Jessi stepped back. "You said it, I didn't."

Soon everybody was fighting with everybody else. The yard was full of crying babies and yelling baby-sitters. Dawn decided to leave. She was sick of the baby parade and it hadn't even happened yet.

Back at the Marshalls', Dawn spent the rest of the day putting together a new costume for Eleanor. She found a blue party dress that used to be Nina's, and she matched it with a pair of blue Mary Jane shoes. She gave Eleanor a new hairstyle — pigtails tied with big ribbons.

"There," she said. "Now you look like a little girl who would be living in a shoe. In that other costume you looked like a clown!"

Eleanor smiled at her and said, "Clown!" (She must have *liked* that other costume.)

But when Mrs. Marshall came home, Dawn told her that the clothes Eleanor had on were perfect for the parade. She asked her to make sure that Eleanor was wearing them on Saturday.

CHAPTER 12

When I woke up on Saturday morning, the first thing I did was look out the window. It was a bright and sunny day, perfect for a parade.

I didn't feel bright and sunny, though.

To be completely honest, I was kind of dreading the parade. I knew our float hadn't turned out well, and I was worried about taking care of so many babies at once. Of course, I was also worried about Andrea's costume — and the "coach" that I had designed for her.

What would Mrs. P. do if Andrea didn't win a prize?

I tried not to think about that. But it was hard to forget the parade. During breakfast, my family kept asking me questions about it.

"Where do you think we should stand for the best view, Kristy?" asked my mom. I suggested a spot.

"Is Slim Peabody really going to be the

grand marshall?" asked Watson. "He was one of my favorite stars when I was a kid. I loved to hear him sing those cowboy songs."

Slim Peabody was supposed to be a celebrity, but he sounded like an old has-been to me. Why couldn't they have gotten somebody like Cam Geary to lead the parade? But I held my tongue and just nodded at Watson. "Yup," I said. "Slim's going to lead the parade."

"I heard that the Girl Scouts made a really professional-looking float," said Sam. "Its theme is 'Save the Animals' and the babies are going to be dressed as endangered species."

"Big deal," I muttered. I went on answering everybody's questions as well as I could, but boy, was I glad when breakfast was over.

"Charlie," I said, when I had finished helping my mom and Watson clean up the kitchen. "Can you take me to the Prezziosos' now? I told Mrs. P. I'd help her get Andrea ready for the parade."

"Me and the Junk Bucket are at your disposal," answered Charlie. "Chauffeur, float-puller, and handyman. All at a special, one-time rate!" He grinned and held out his hand, rubbing his fingers and thumb together. "Pay up!" he said. "I want my fee in advance."

I gave him the money we'd agreed on. (The BSC members had voted to take it out of the treasury.) It wasn't much. I knew Charlie was really helping me out of the kindness of his heart. "Okay, let's get going," I said.

When we arrived at the Prezziosos', Mrs. P. was, predictably, in a tizzy. Andrea's costume was half on and half off — and the half that was off was scattered all over the first floor of the house.

And then I saw what Mrs. P. was wearing. Did you ever have to pretend you were having a coughing fit in order to cover up a giggle that slipped out? That's what I had to do. Mrs. P. was dressed up as one of the "Queen's" guards. She was wearing this red uniform (she must have rented it from a costume place) with big black boots and one of those high, high furry black hats that look like an animal nesting on top of your head. Fake medals were pinned all over her chest.

I couldn't even look at Charlie, who was waiting in his car. I knew he could see her from where he was sitting, and I knew if we looked at each other we would burst out laughing.

While Mrs. P. ran upstairs to finish dressing, I got Andrea ready. I picked up her ruff from where it hung over a lampshade and slipped it over her head. "There you go, Your Highness!" I said. Then I looked around for the rest of her costume. When she was all set, I called to Mrs. P. to ask where the "coach" was.

"Back porch," she yelled from her bedroom. "But wait a minute. I want you to check something for me." She ran downstairs. "What do you think of my makeup?" she asked.

What did I think? I thought it looked like Jenny had been the makeup artist. "It looks — great!" I said, trying to sound enthusiastic.

"Thanks," she said. "Jenny helped a lot."

I knew it.

After I'd approved Mrs. P.'s makeup, I checked on the stroller I'd decorated for Andrea. As soon as I saw it, I knew that Jenny had "helped" with it, too. I had decorated the stroller to look like a small but royal coach, with wheels made out of gold-painted cardboard. A cardboard horse was fastened to the front, and it really did look like the horse was pulling the coach. Then that fancy fabric was draped over the coach, giving it a royal look.

Jenny, however, had added a slew of stickers, pasted on every which way. And none of the stickers had anything to do with the "Queen Andrea" theme. There were Care Bear stickers and Teenage Mutant Ninja Turtle stickers and Barbie stickers. Jenny had raided her collection.

"It's beautiful, isn't it?" Jenny was standing

behind me, gazing at the stroller.

What could I say?

"Beautiful," I answered. "You really went to town with those stickers, didn't you?" I couldn't be mad at Jenny. I could tell that she was proud of what she'd done, and I figured that the stickers wouldn't show up enough to be seen from the reviewing stand.

"Let's bring the Queen's coach to the front yard now, okay?" I said.

Jenny helped me with the stroller. One of the big cardboard wheels got a little bent, but I was able to fold it back to its original shape. And one of the horse's ears got torn, but I hoped nobody would notice.

I looked over at Charlie, who was still sitting in his car. His arms were folded over his chest. He looked a little impatient. And I had to go home, anyway. I had to get my costume together and dress Emily in hers.

"I think eveything's ready, Mrs. P.," I called up the stairs.

Mrs. P. appeared on the second-floor landing. She was using a curling iron on her hair — why, I don't know, since it was going to be under that big hat — and she waved good-bye.

"Thanks for everything, Kristy," she said. "Wish us luck!"

"Good luck!" I called. (They were going to need it.) "See you at the parade," I added to Jenny. She was going to be standing in a special spot, along with Becca and Jamie and some other kids who were too old to march (or ride) in the parade. Our associate members, Logan and Shannon, had been hired to watch the group of children until the parade was over.

Back at home, I rushed around madly trying to figure out what to wear. I was supposed to be dressed as the Old Woman. Don't ask me how that had been decided, because I have no idea. Probably, no one else wanted to be the Old Woman.

I put on a frumpy-looking blouse and one of my mom's long skirts. I tied on an old apron. Then I drew some wrinkles on my face with eyebrow pencil. I looked in the mirror. "Not bad," I said, "for a five-minute costume."

I wrestled Emily into her pink, clown outfit. She didn't seem all that thrilled to be wearing it — in fact, she had started wailing the minute I brought it out. Even so, as soon as she was dressed, I picked her up and headed downstairs. "Ta-daaa!" I said, as I entered the living room, where everybody was waiting.

There was a long silence.

Finally, Mom found her voice. "Very nice,

Kristy," she said. "But why is Emily dressed like a clown?"

I shrugged and shook my head. "Don't ask me," I said. "It wasn't my idea." I turned to Charlie. "Ready to take an Old Woman and a clown over to Claudia's?" I asked.

"Ready," he answered.

I headed out the door carrying Emily. My family waved good-bye. They'd be leaving soon, too, to stake out a good spot on the parade route. Watson was bringing the camcorder.

I put Emily into her car seat, and we were off to Claud's house. It was time to hook the float to Charlie's car. When we pulled up, Charlie honked the horn and Claudia ran out. She was wearing a flowery dress that had once belonged to her grandmother Mimi. I guess that was supposed to be her costume.

"I'm all ready, and so's the float," she said. She opened the garage door, and there it was.

"Whoa!" said Charlie when he saw the float. He slumped down in his seat. "You've got to be kidding. I'm supposed to pull that — that *thing* behind my car?"

Claudia put her hands on her hips. "It's not *that* bad, Charlie," she said. "Besides, we're paying you good money to do it."

"Right," mumbled Charlie.

"Okay," I said, jumping out of the car. "Let's get it hitched up. C'mon. It'll look fine."

I was wrong. So sue me.

The float looked as awful as ever once it was hitched to the Junk Bucket. It was just a giant reddish blob with long, snaky things hanging off it.

"What are *those?*" asked Charlie, pointing to one.

"Shoelaces," said Claud, firmly.

"Oh."

That was when I knew for sure that our float was a disaster. "Do you think it's too late — ?" I started to ask Claudia, but she interrupted me.

"To call the parents of all those babies and cancel?" she asked. "Kristy, are you out of your mind? Of course it's too late. We're just going to have to make the best of it."

Charlie, meanwhile, had gone around to the back of the car and was rummaging in the trunk.

"What are you looking for?" I asked him.

"This," he answered, holding up an old, floppy hat that he sometimes wore when he and Sam went fishing. He put it on. Then he slammed the trunk shut. He walked around the car and slid into the driver's seat. Next he started to poke around in the glove compartment.

"*Now* what are you looking for?" I asked. I still hadn't figured out why he was wearing that ratty old hat.

"These," he answered, putting on a pair of mirrored sunglasses that someone had once left in his car. "Now I'm all set," he said, grinning. "There's no way anybody will recognize me now."

"Charlie!" Claud and I yelled together. I knew then how bad the float really looked.

We drove to the parade route (slowly, because the float was kind of drifting across the road) and met the other club members at the spot we'd decided on. All of the babies were there already, and some of their parents were still hanging around, looking kind of worried.

None of the club members' costumes had anything in common. (Of course.) Dawn was dressed sort of like a beachcomber, Mary Anne looked like Raggedy Anne (she was using parts of an old Halloween costume), and Jessi was wearing some sort of ballet getup. Stacey had on an old sweat shirt that said, "New York — The Big Apple," and Mallory was dressed as she normally is.

Then there were the babies in their silly costumes. At least they looked like they belonged together. Except for Eleanor, who was wearing her party dress.

112

Our float was a disaster, and each of us thought this was somebody *else's* fault. Within about two seconds, not one member of the BSC was speaking to the others.

What a mess.

CHAPTER 13

I was glaring at Dawn. Why did she have to dress Eleanor differently from all the other babies? Dawn was glaring at Claudia — I guess because of the way the float looked. Claudia was glaring at Stacey.

Everybody was looking pretty angry.

But the parade was about to start, and we were part of the parade, whether we liked it or not.

I passed out the sunblock I'd brought, while Mallory went around fastening the babies' sunbonnets. So what if my friends and I weren't speaking to each other? So what if our float looked like The Creature From Another Planet? We had to take care of those babies.

"Okay, folks!" I heard a voice over the loudspeaker. "Let's saddle up and move 'em out!"

Oh, how corny.

At least *I* thought it was corny. I noticed that Jessi and Mal were gazing in rapture at

Slim Peabody. He was sitting on a big white horse at the front of the parade, which was about a block away from where we were. His saddle was trimmed with silver, and he was wearing a cowboy outfit.

"Wow," breathed Jessi, looking at the horse. "Look at that beautiful animal."

Mallory nodded. "He's gorgeous," she murmured.

Then they remembered that they weren't speaking to each other, and their mouths snapped shut.

Working quickly, we settled the babies in bouncers or on the blankets. They were spread around the shoe. I had kind of pictured them peeking *out* of the shoe — but I knew there was no point in saying anything now. Especially since I wasn't speaking to Claudia, anyway.

At least Claudia had realized that we would need something to keep the babies from falling "overboard." She had built a little guardrail around the float. I settled myself behind it, with Emily in my lap. I had promised Mrs. Salem that I'd be responsible for Ricky and Rose, too, so they were propped up nearby.

When the float in front of us began to move, I gave Charlie the signal. We were on our way.

Before we had gotten started, I'd been too busy to be nervous. But now that the float was moving, my stomach felt jumpy. I wondered how "Queen Andrea" looked, and whether she'd win the prize that Mrs. P. wanted so badly. I wondered if the float would last the parade route without falling apart. And I wondered if I was going to be able to stand the humiliation of having hundreds of people watch me ride by.

I could barely look at the crowds lining the street. Watson and Mom were there, somewhere, filming the event for posterity. That was one video I knew *I'd* never watch.

As we rolled along, I sneaked a peek at some of the spectators. They'd been applauding and cheering for the floats before us, but they looked a little confused by our float. I couldn't blame them. The fact is, that without these big signs that Claudia had made to hang on the sides of the float, I'm sure no one would ever have known what it was supposed to be.

She'd made the signs in a hurry, and it showed. The one that hung from my side of the float said, THEIR WAS AN OLD WOMMAN WHO LIVED IN A SHO. The other one said, THAIR WAS AN OLD WOMANN WHO LIVED IN A SHUE. Nobody had had time to check Claud's spelling.

I thought I heard people laughing, but I

trained my eyes straight ahead and tried not to think about it. At least the babies were behaving. Not one of them was crying — so far. And, even though none of us baby-sitters was speaking to the others, at least we weren't fighting out loud.

It could have been worse.

I tried to relax. I was stuck on that float until the parade was over, so I knew I might as well make the best of it. I looked up ahead, trying to see how some of the other floats were decorated.

The one in front of us was *very* professional-looking. It was a living merry-go-round! From under a canopy dropped a circle of poles. At the bottom of each pole was a grown-up holding a baby —and each baby was dressed in a really terrific animal costume. The circle moved around and around in time to the music that was playing from a tape player in the middle of the float.

The crowd *loved* it.

Behind us was the float Sam had heard about, the one the Girl Scouts had made. It was decorated to look like a tropical rain forest, and each of the babies was supposed to be an endangered species. On the front was a big sign that said, SAVE THE ANIMALS. The float looked nice, but I don't think the babies were all that happy. They were wearing these special animal masks as part of their costumes, and a lot of the babies were crying from behind the masks.

When I craned my neck, I could see some of the Single Stroller entries way behind us. I knew that Mrs. P. and Andrea were back there, even though I couldn't make them out. I wondered if the other strollers were as wild and gaudy as Mrs. P.'s. I had a feeling she'd gone a little overboard with her Queen Andrea idea.

There were also entries in which kids were being pulled along in wagons or pushed in little go-carts. I hadn't gotten a good look at any of them, except one — Little Miss Muffet. It was really good. It made me wish we'd stuck to a simpler nursery rhyme.

By the time the parade hit the main route, all the bands that were marching with us had begun to play. I could hear a banjo band in back of us, and I knew a big marching band was leading the parade. But guess which band was marching nearest to us?

The bagpipe band.

I *hate* bagpipes. Maybe you've never heard them, so I'll try to describe how they sound. Imagine twenty mean cats fighting over a single piece of fish.

That's how bagpipes sound to me.

I looked at Mary Anne. She hates bagpipes, too. I gave her a little smile, but she just glared at me. Her hands were over her ears.

Then I heard a voice yelling over the caterwauling bagpipes. "Hey, Thomas! What's that you're pulling? It looks like a mutant marshmallow!"

Oh, no. Charlie's friends had spotted him through his disguise. I saw a crowd of boys standing on the sidewalk. They were pointing at the float and laughing. I guess they had recognized the Junk Bucket. (Charlie slumped down in his seat, trying to pretend that he somehow wasn't involved.)

"Hey, Thomas!" yelled another one of the boys. "What are you going to do with your prize money?"

Oh, ha-ha.

I could almost see the steam coming out of Charlie's ears. I was going to be hearing about this for a long, long time. I started to figure out how many nights I would have to take out the garbage for him in order to make up for the parade.

Then the worst thing in the world happened.

Just as we were about to go past the group of boys, the crowd parted slightly and I could see that some girls were with them, too. None of them called out to Charlie — but they were whispering and giggling as they looked at our float. Even from where I was sitting, I could see the back of Charlie's neck turning bright red.

I was really in for it now.

The parade seemed to be moving at a crawl. Most parades end before you want them to, but not this one. It seemed to have been going on for years. We crawled past the spot where Watson and Mom were standing. They cheered and waved. Then we passed Shannon and Logan and the kids they were sitting for. We got a big cheer from them, too.

By that time, the babies were tired of being good. Squirt had started to cry when the bagpipes began playing; they'd stopped, but he hadn't. Ricky and Rose were bawling, too.

Dawn had her hands full with Eleanor, who kept trying to escape from the float. Eleanor's party dress was smudged with red paint, and the bows in her hair had come loose.

Babies were crawling all over the float. None of them wanted to stay put. As soon as Stacey or Claudia got one settled, another one would start to take off.

Then Emily complained of a tummy ache. She was carsick. (Floatsick?)

By the time we passed the reviewing stand, I couldn't even bring myself to smile and wave at the judges. I didn't care anymore about winning a prize. All I wanted was for the parade to be over.

CHAPTER 14

Finally the parade wound up in the little park near the shopping center. What a relief! No more riding past all those smiling faces. No more waving.

But the day wasn't over yet.

First, we had to wait for the rest of the parade to reach the park. Then would come the time for the judges to announce their decisions and hand out prizes.

Obviously we wouldn't be winning any prizes — unless they were giving out a prize for "Worst Float." But I did want to find out who *had* won. Especially in the Stroller Division.

"I'm outta here!" said Charlie, as soon as he'd parked the car. He climbed out of the Junk Bucket and slammed the door.

"But Charlie — " I wanted to make sure he'd be back. Eventually.

"No 'buts,' Kristy. I don't want to have anything else to do with this parade. I'll come back when it's all over."

There was no point in arguing with him. "Okay, Charlie," I said. "See you later."

I turned back to see what everybody else was doing. My friends were still sitting on the float. The babies had settled down again. Some of them had even fallen asleep. Each baby-sitter was holding a baby in her lap. However, nobody looked as though she were ready to make up, and I wasn't about to be the one to start.

We just watched the rest of the parade trickle into the park. There were some amazing floats. On any other day we would have been talking about them, pointing out special things and laughing at the funny ones.

But that day, we weren't talking to each other. So instead, we talked to the babies we were holding.

"Look at that, Emily!" I said, pointing at a float that had just turned in to the park. The theme was *Star Wars*. The float was decorated to look like a spaceship, and there were four babies on board. One was dressed like Princess Leia, braids and all. Another was supposed to be Luke Skywalker. He was carrying a plastic sword that was bigger than he was. Then there was Han Solo, looking like a real swashbuckler, and a furry Chewbacca.

"Funny!" said Emily, chuckling. That's one of the words she's just learned.

I pointed out the *Star Wars* float to Ricky and Rose, too — but they didn't seem too impressed. Ricky just yawned, and Rose gave a little burp. They were just too young to appreciate it.

"Hey, Squirt," said Jessi. "Look!" I sneaked a peek at the float that Jessi was pointing to.

"Dothy!" said Squirt happily.

"That's right," replied Jessi. "Dorothy and her friends the Tin Man, the Scarecrow, and the Cowardly Lion. And I see the Wizard, too!"

It was a pretty great float. Somebody had spent a lot of time making costumes for those babies. I felt even more embarrassed than before when I thought of how quickly I had thrown my Old Woman outfit together.

Finally the floats stopped arriving, and we started to see the strollers, wagons, and go-carts roll in. A lot of the babies in those divisions were asleep, but you could still get an idea of what their costumes were.

Right away, I felt ridiculous for having even wondered if Andrea's stroller was too gaudy. People really went to town when they decorated these things! I never saw so many ribbons, bows, and sequins in one place before. *Now* I started to wonder if Andrea's stroller was too boring! If I hadn't been in public, I would have groaned out loud. I didn't think Queen Andrea had any more chance of winning in her division that we had in ours.

"Wow!" I heard Dawn say. "Look at that, Eleanor." Eleanor was grinning and bouncing up and down. I followed her eyes and saw a mother pulling a wagon that was decorated to look like one of my favorite books: *Good Night Moon*. (It's about getting ready for bed and saying good night to everything in your room. Kids *love* it, and it's a great way to get them to go to bed.)

The wagon was made to look like a little bed, and the boy who was lying in it must have been about two and a half. His favorite toys were around him. And there was a "window" (made out of cardboard and plastic wrap) running up the side of the wagon, with a big yellow moon hanging in it. It was the cutest thing!

After about a half hour, just when I was feeling as if I couldn't possibly sit on that float for another minute, Slim Peabody stepped onto the stage that had been set up and tapped on the microphone. A piercing screech rang out, and everybody quieted down right away.

"Just testing, pardners!" said Slim.

Oh, please.

"We sure are glad you could all come out

for this little parade today," he went on, now that he'd gotten everybody's attention. "Me and Buster were proud to be a part of it."

Buster? Oh, that must be the horse's name. Of course. Silly me.

"How 'bout if we give all these little ladies and gents a great big hand?" he asked the audience. The spectators applauded loudly. The park was pretty jammed by then.

I figured that maybe about six of these people were clapping for us — and only because they knew us.

"I know you're all just rarin' to know who won the prizes in each division," continued Slim.

Yes! I thought. Let's get on with it. I couldn't wait to get off that float and out of my costume.

"But first," he went on, "the parade committee asked me to entertain you while the judges confer."

Oh, no. Anything but —

Slim pulled out a guitar and strummed on it. Then he began to yodel and sing loudly into the mike. *I'm an old cowhand from the Rio Grande.*

Maybe way back when Watson was a fan of his, Slim could carry a tune. But I'm here to tell you that those days were long gone. Slim tortured us with about ten more minutes of cowboy songs before one of the judges bounded up onto the stage and politely cut him off.

"Thank you so much, Mr. Peabody," he said.

"Call me Slim," said Slim.

"Let's give Slim a big Stoneybrook hand!" said the judge, turning to the audience. I think everybody applauded as enthusiastically as they did because they were hoping Slim's show was really over. I know that's why I was clapping.

"How 'bout an encore?" I heard Slim ask the judge. He was close enough to the mike so that we all heard it. I held my breath.

"I think these folks are eager to hear about their winners, Mr. — Slim," said the judge. Slim waved and headed off the stage. "And now," said the judge, "it's time to announce the winners of this year's Stoneybrook Baby Parade!"

I wanted to die. This was going to be pure torture. Not only were we not going to get a prize, but Andrea wasn't, either. The parade was a complete disaster. I looked around for Charlie. If only he would show up now and drive me home!

But Charlie was nowhere to be seen.

The judge started to announce the winners. "In the Go-cart Division," he said, "The winner of Third Prize is Kevin Davis, for his depiction of Rambo!"

There was lots of cheering for Kevin. I'd missed that Rambo cart, and to tell the truth, I didn't care.

The judge went on, announcing third-, second-, and first-place winners in all the categories. When he announced the Float Division, I held my breath. What if I was wrong and somehow we had won Third Prize? (I knew there was no chance we'd do any better than that.) I'd have to go up onstage and accept the ribbon in my awful costume.

"And the third-place winner is — "

I closed my eyes.

"The Wizard of Oz!" he finished. "Congratulations to the Morse family." The prize-giving went on and on. The merry-go-round won first prize in the floats, and I was glad.

Finally the judge announced the Stroller Division. I crossed my fingers, my toes, and my arms, wishing as hard as I could that Andrea would win. The judge announced the third-place winner. It wasn't Andrea. He announced the second-place winner. Not Andrea.

"And First Prize in this division goes to Andrea Prezzioso — or Queen Andrea!" said the judge, smiling.

I heaved a great sigh as I watched Mrs. P. carry Andrea up to the stage to receive her ribbon. My job was safe — even if the Baby-sitters Club broke up tomorrow, which looked entirely possible.

As soon as the judging was over, parents started arriving at our float to pick up their babies. They looked pretty relieved to see that their children were still in one piece. I don't think any of them had actually expected to win a prize, so they weren't disappointed.

Mrs. P. rushed over to me, smiling happily. "Thank you *so much*," she said. "Isn't it wonderful?" She showed me Andrea's blue ribbon. Andrea was asleep in her stroller. Jenny was holding her mother's hand.

"We won, Kristy!" she said. "Just like you said we would."

Lucky for me.

As the last baby was being picked up, Charlie came back. My ex-friends and I piled into the Junk Bucket and, with the float trailing behind us, Charlie drove us home. Needless to say, there was no talking along the way.

Finally Charlie, Emily, and I were the only ones left in the car. "What do you want me to do with the float?" asked Charlie.

"Take it to the dump," I answered. "Please."

CHAPTER 15

When Charlie pulled up outside our house, I unbuckled Emily from her car seat and lifted her out of the car.

Charlie was still sitting behind the wheel. "Do you really want me to take it to the dump?" he asked, gesturing to the float. It sat behind the car, all lumpy and red.

"I do," I answered. I never wanted to see that thing again.

My brother shrugged. "Okay," he said. He waved good-bye and pulled away from the curb.

"Make sure it gets crushed in the compacter!" I called after him. Then I took Emily inside. The house was quiet. Mom must have gone out shopping and Watson was in his study. Nannie was sitting in the living room, reading.

"How was the parade, sweetie?" she asked.

"Just be glad you had a bowling tournament

today and you couldn't come," I answered. "It was a disaster. At least, our float was. Actually, the rest of the parade was pretty good."

Nannie smiled at me. "I'll be glad to watch Emily for awhile," she said. "You look tired."

"Thanks," I replied. "I'll just get her out of this costume, and then I'll bring her down to you." I carried Emily upstairs and took off her costume. Emily had certainly been good-natured during the parade. "You're the best, Miss Em," I said, kissing her nose.

She giggled and kissed me back.

I found a clean sundress for Emily and buttoned her into it. She looked happy to be out of that clown costume. I threw the costume into the laundry basket, figuring she might be able to use it next Halloween. Then I took Emily back downstairs.

"Come here, honey," said Nannie, spreading her arms wide. Emily ran over to her, laughing. "Okay, Kristy," said Nannie. "You're free now."

Free to do what I really wanted to do: go to my room and think. I headed upstairs again and changed out of my costume. Then I lay across my bed. I wanted to figure out what had gone so terribly wrong with our float. Usually our club projects turn out pretty well, but this one had bombed.

It didn't take me long to understand what

had happened. The reason we didn't make a better float was because we hadn't worked *together*. Everybody had gone her separate way, each thinking she knew what was best. We hadn't been communicating at all. And now we were all mad at each other.

It was time to start talking — even if it was too late to save our float. I decided to call Mary Anne and apologize. Since she's my best friend, I wanted to be sure to make up with her first.

I went to the phone in the hall and dialed her number. She picked up the receiver after one ring.

"Hello?" she said.

"Hi, Mary Anne? It's me, Kristy. I'm calling to apologize. I don't want us to be mad at each other anymore."

"This is *so* weird," said Mary Anne. "When you called, I had my hand on the phone. I was going to call *you*."

"Really?" I asked.

"Really," she answered. "Dawn and I made up as soon as we got home. I *hate* it when we're all fighting. And I think everybody else is probably making up, too. It's ridiculous for us to be so mad about that stupid old float."

I agreed with Mary Anne.

"And you know what?" she went on. "Dawn and I realized that we weren't really that mad at each other. It was more that we were embarrassed — about the float."

"I know what you mean," I said. "It *was* pretty embarrassing, wasn't it?" I started to giggle, and so did Mary Anne. Soon we were laughing so hard we couldn't stop.

"I thought I would *die* when Slim Peabody was singing," I said.

"I know. And what about those bagpipes?" Suddenly I couldn't remember why we had ever been so mad at each other in the first place.

After I got off the phone with Mary Anne, I spent some time calling the other members of the BSC. Dawn and Mary Anne had been right; everybody was more than ready to make up.

"Let's talk about this at Monday's meeting," said Stacey, when I called her. "Maybe we can learn something from this."

"Good idea," I said.

That night at dinner, Mom and Watson wanted to talk about the parade. "Wasn't that merry-go-round float wonderful?" asked Mom.

"It sure was," I said. "Too bad we were right behind it."

Watson smiled at me. "Oh, come on, Kristy. Your float wasn't so bad," he said.

"Yes it was!" exclaimed Charlie. "But now

that 'Shoe' is the size of a *shoe box*. It was really satisfying to watch it get crushed."

"I'm sorry those guys recognized you," I said to Charlie. I didn't even want to *mention* the girls.

"No big deal," he said. "I'll get over it." He punched me lightly on the shoulder. "Just don't ever ask me to pull one of your club's floats again."

"Don't worry," I said. "I don't think we'll be entering any parades for awhile."

By Monday, the parade was just a memory. I spent the early part of the afternoon sitting for Jenny and Andrea. By then, I had gotten used to taking care of both of them — in fact, it was starting to be fun.

Andrea's prize ribbon had been mounted on the wall above her crib, and Mrs. P. was late getting out of the house because she "just had" to show me the parade pictures she'd asked a friend to take. She thanked me again and again for my help.

"I was glad to do it," I said. I wasn't lying, either. I'd had fun decorating Andrea's stroller. I may not be as good an artist as Claudia, but I had to admit that I had done a pretty good job on that coach.

When I was done at the Prezziosos', I headed for Claudia's house. It was time for our club meeting. As usual, I was early, but it wasn't long before the others started to trickle in.

"Hi, Stacey," I said when she stuck her head in the doorway. She smiled at me and sat down at Claud's desk. Claud was already in place on her bed.

Jessi and Mallory arrived together and plopped on the floor. Jessi had a magazine with her, and she and Mal were tearing out the perfume ads and rubbing the scented paper on their wrists.

"I like this one, don't you?" asked Mal, thrusting her wrist toward me.

I sniffed and coughed. "Nice," I said. "It's kind of . . . strong, though, isn't it?"

"I think it's really *rich*-smelling," said Jessi. "Like what you'd wear if you lived in Beverly Hills or something."

By then, Dawn and Mary Anne had arrived, and Claud was busy rummaging around under her pillow. I had a feeling I knew what she was looking for.

"I *thought* I'd saved something for the meeting," she said, pulling out a bag of mini chocolate bars. "Who likes Snickers?" She passed the bag to Jessi and Mal. "And I've got something here for the health nuts, too," she went on, searching under the bed. "Low-salt Triscuits!" She tossed the box to Dawn.

135

Just then, I noticed out of the corner of my eye that the digital clock had clicked to 5:30. "Order!" I said. Jessi and Mal put away their magazine. The meeting had begun.

Since it was a Monday, dues were the first order of business. "Cough it up, you guys!" said Stacey happily, passing around the envelope. She just loves to collect that money.

"How much is in the treasury?" I asked.

Stacey counted it in a matter of seconds. I don't know how she does it so fast. "Well," she answered, "we've got enough for a pizza party. But not enough for extra topping. It looks like we spent the pepperoni money on the *you*-know-what."

"The float?" I asked. "You can say it. It's all in the past, now."

"Thank heaven," said Claud. "What a disaster. You know, I realized something. A big project like that just can't work without cooperation."

"Right," said Dawn. "A little give-and-take."

"Communication!" said Mary Anne.

"Working together," added Jessi and Mal.

"Okay," I said. "So at least *one* good thing came out of the baby parade. We learned an important lesson."

The phone rang then. It was Mrs. Salem. She needed a sitter for Ricky and Rose. And not too long after that, we got another phone call. It was Mrs. Gold, another mother from our class, wanting to hire us to watch her two-month-old baby.

"I heard from Mrs. Salem what a wonderful job you did with the babies on your float," she said to me.

After we'd set up the jobs, I looked around Claud's room and smiled at my friends. "I guess that's *three* good things that came out of the parade," I said. "One lesson and two new clients!"

About the Author

ANN M. MARTIN did *a lot* of baby-sitting when she was growing up in Princeton, New Jersey. Now her favorite baby-sitting charge is her cat, Mouse, who lives with her in her Manhattan apartment.

Ann Martin's Apple Paperbacks include *Yours Turly, Shirley; Ten Kids, No Pets; With You and Without You; Bummer Summer;* and all the other books in the Baby-sitters Club series.

She is a former editor of books for children, and was graduated from Smith College. She likes ice cream, the beach, and *I Love Lucy;* and she hates to cook.

Look for #46

MARY ANNE MISSES LOGAN

An announcement came over the speaker system. "Attention, all eighth-graders. Attention, all eighth-graders. Your author-study project begins today. The lists of groups, and the authors to be studied, have been posted outside the office on the first floor. Please check the lists on your way home today. Thank you."

My heart was pounding. Now I was just waiting for —

BR-R-R-RING!

The final bell.

In a flurry of activity, my classmates and I gathered up our books and flew out of the room. Most kids were heading for their lockers. But I ran straight downstairs to the office. A few other kids had done the same thing. I was glad I'd arrived early. Already, it was difficult to see the wall.

It took me a minute or two to figure out

how to find my group. The number 42 was printed next to my name on the eighth-grade class list.

"Forty-two," I murmured.

I stepped over to another list and peered at it until I found 42.

There it is, I thought. The people in group 42 study . . . Megan Rinehart!

I was ecstatic. This *must* be a sign of good luck. I adore Megan Rinehart's books. Imagine being assigned to study them. And her. It would be more like fun than work.

I glanced under Megan Rinehart's name to find out who was in my group.

And my stomach flip-flopped. I absolutely could not believe what I saw.

I would be studying Megan Rinehart with Miranda Shillaber, Pete Black (*they* were okay), . . . and Logan.

Logan Bruno.

Read all the books
in the Baby-sitters Club series
by Ann M. Martin

1 *Kristy's Great Idea*
Kristy's great idea is to start *The Baby-sitters Club*!

2 *Claudia and the Phantom Phone Calls*
Someone mysterious is calling Claudia!

3 *The Truth About Stacey*
Stacey's different . . . and it's harder on her than anyone knows.

4 *Mary Anne Saves the Day*
Mary Anne is tired of being treated like a baby. It's time to take charge!

5 *Dawn and the Impossible Three*
Dawn thought she'd be baby-sitting — not *monster*-sitting!

6 *Kristy's Big Day*
Kristy's a baby-sitter — and a bridesmaid, too!

7 *Claudia and Mean Janine*
Claudia's big sister is super smart . . . and super *mean*.

8 *Boy-Crazy Stacey*
Stacey's too busy being *boy-crazy* to baby-sit!

9 *The Ghost at Dawn's House*
Creaking stairs, a secret passage — there must be a ghost at Dawn's house!

#10 *Logan Likes Mary Anne!*
Mary Anne has a crush on a *boy* baby-sitter!

#11 *Kristy and the Snobs*
The kids in Kristy's new neighborhood are S-N-O-B-S!

#12 *Claudia and the New Girl*
Claudia might give up the club — and it's all Ashley's fault!

#13 *Good-bye Stacey, Good-bye*
Oh, no! Stacey McGill is moving back to New York!

#14 *Hello, Mallory*
Is Mallory Pike good enough to join the club?

#15 *Little Miss Stoneybrook . . . and Dawn*
Everyone in Stoneybrook has gone beauty-pageant crazy!

#16 *Jessi's Secret Language*
Jessi's new charge is teaching her a *secret language*.

#17 *Mary Anne's Bad-Luck Mystery*
Will Mary Anne's bad luck ever go away?

#18 *Stacey's Mistake*
Has Stacey made a big mistake by inviting the Baby-sitters to New York City?

#19 *Claudia and the Bad Joke*
Claudia is headed for trouble when she baby-sits for a practical joker.

#20 *Kristy and the Walking Disaster*
Can Kristy's Krushers beat Bart's Bashers?

#21 *Mallory and the Trouble With Twins*
Sitting for the Arnold twins is double trouble!

#22 *Jessi Ramsey, Pet-sitter*
Jessi has to baby-sit for a house full of . . . *pets!*

#23 *Dawn on the Coast*
Could Dawn be a California girl for good?

#24 *Kristy and the Mother's Day Surprise*
Emily Michelle is the big surprise!

#25 *Mary Anne and the Search for Tigger*
Tigger is missing! Has he been catnapped?

#26 *Claudia and the Sad Good-bye*
Claudia never thought she'd have to say good-bye
to her grandmother.

#27 *Jessi and the Superbrat*
Jessi gets to baby-sit for a TV star!

#28 *Welcome Back, Stacey!*
Stacey's moving again . . . back to Stoneybrook!

#29 *Mallory and the Mystery Diary*
Only Mal can solve the mystery in the old diary.

#30 *Mary Anne and the Great Romance*
Mary Anne's father and Dawn's mother are getting
married!

#31 *Dawn's Wicked Stepsister*
Dawn thought having a stepsister was going to be
fun. Was she ever wrong!

#32 Kristy and the Secret of Susan
Even Kristy can't learn all of Susan's secrets.

#33 Claudia and the Great Search
There are *no* baby pictures of Claudia. Could she have been . . . adopted?!

#34 Mary Anne and Too Many Boys
Will a summer romance come between Mary Anne and Logan?

#35 Stacey and the Mystery of Stoneybrook
Stacey discovers a *haunted house* in Stoneybrook!

#36 Jessi's Baby-sitter
How could Jessi's parents have gotten a *baby-sitter* for her?

#37 Dawn and the Older Boy
Will Dawn's heart be broken by an older boy?

#38 Kristy's Mystery Admirer
Someone is sending Kristy *love notes!*

#39 Poor Mallory!
Mallory's dad has lost his job, but the Pike kids are coming to the rescue!

#40 Claudia and the Middle School Mystery
Can the Baby-sitters find out who the cheater is at SMS?

#41 Mary Anne vs. Logan
Mary Anne thought she and Logan would be together forever. . . .

#42 Jessi and the Dance School Phantom
Someone — or some*thing* — wants Jessi out of the show.

#43 *Stacey's Emergency*
The Baby-sitters are so worried. Something's wrong with Stacey.

#44 *Dawn and the Big Sleepover*
A hundred kids, thirty pizzas — it's Dawn's biggest baby-sitting job ever!

#45 *Kristy and the Baby Parade*
Will the Baby-sitters' float take first prize in the Stoneybrook Baby Parade?

#46 *Mary Anne Misses Logan*
But does Logan miss *her*?

Super Specials:
 # 1 *Baby-sitters on Board!*
Guess who's going on a dream vacation? The Baby-sitters!

 # 2 *Baby-sitters' Summer Vacation*
Good-bye, Stoneybrook . . . hello, Camp Mohawk!

 # 3 *Baby-sitters' Winter Vacation*
The Baby-sitters are off for a week of winter fun!

 # 4 *Baby-sitters' Island Adventure*
Two of the Baby-sitters are shipwrecked!

 # 5 *California Girls!*
A winning lottery ticket sends the Baby-sitters to *California!*

 # 6 *New York, New York!*
Bloomingdale's, the Hard Rock Cafe — the BSC is going to see it all!

THE BABY-SITTERS CLUB ®

by Ann M. Martin

The Baby-sitters' business is booming! And that gets Stacey, Kristy, Claudia, and the rest of The Baby-sitters Club members in all kinds of adventures...at school, with boys, and, of course, baby-sitting!

Something new and exciting happens in every Baby-sitters Club book. Collect and read them all!

☐ MG43388-1	#1	**Kristy's Great Idea**	$2.95
☐ MG43513-2	#2	**Claudia and the Phantom Phone Calls**	$2.95
☐ MG43511-6	#3	**The Truth About Stacey**	$2.95
☐ MG43512-4	#4	**Mary Anne Saves the Day**	$2.95
☐ MG43720-8	#5	**Dawn and the Impossible Three**	$2.95
☐ MG43899-9	#6	**Kristy's Big Day**	$2.95
☐ MG43719-4	#7	**Claudia and Mean Janine**	$2.95
☐ MG43509-4	#8	**Boy-Crazy Stacey**	$2.95
☐ MG43508-6	#9	**The Ghost at Dawn's House**	$2.95
☐ MG43387-3	#10	**Logan Likes Mary Anne!**	$2.95
☐ MG43660-0	#11	**Kristy and the Snobs**	$2.95
☐ MG43721-6	#12	**Claudia and the New Girl**	$2.95
☐ MG43386-5	#13	**Good-bye Stacey, Good-bye**	$2.95
☐ MG43385-7	#14	**Hello, Mallory**	$2.95
☐ MG43717-8	#15	**Little Miss Stoneybrook...and Dawn**	$2.95
☐ MG44234-1	#16	**Jessi's Secret Language**	$2.95
☐ MG43659-7	#17	**Mary Anne's Bad-Luck Mystery**	$2.95
☐ MG43718-6	#18	**Stacey's Mistake**	$2.95
☐ MG43510-8	#19	**Claudia and the Bad Joke**	$2.95
☐ MG43722-4	#20	**Kristy and the Walking Disaster**	$2.95
☐ MG43507-8	#21	**Mallory and the Trouble with Twins**	$2.95
☐ MG43658-9	#22	**Jessi Ramsey, Pet-sitter**	$2.95
☐ MG43900-6	#23	**Dawn on the Coast**	$2.95
☐ MG43506-X	#24	**Kristy and the Mother's Day Surprise**	$2.95
☐ MG43347-4	#25	**Mary Anne and the Search for Tigger**	$2.95
☐ MG42503-X	#26	**Claudia and the Sad Good-bye**	$2.95

More titles... ▶

The Baby-sitters Club titles continued...

❑ MG42503-1	#27 **Jessi and the Superbrat**	$2.95
❑ MG42501-3	#28 **Welcome Back, Stacey!**	$2.95
❑ MG42500-5	#29 **Mallory and the Mystery Diary**	$2.95
❑ MG42498-X	#30 **Mary Anne and the Great Romance**	$2.95
❑ MG42497-1	#31 **Dawn's Wicked Stepsister**	$2.95
❑ MG42496-3	#32 **Kristy and the Secret of Susan**	$2.95
❑ MG42495-5	#33 **Claudia and the Great Search**	$2.95
❑ MG42494-7	#34 **Mary Anne and Too Many Boys**	$2.95
❑ MG42508-0	#35 **Stacey and the Mystery of Stoneybrook**	$2.95
❑ MG43565-5	#36 **Jessi's Baby-sitter**	$2.95
❑ MG43566-3	#37 **Dawn and the Older Boy**	$2.95
❑ MG43567-1	#38 **Kristy's Mystery Admirer**	$2.95
❑ MG43568-X	#39 **Poor Mallory!**	$2.95
❑ MG44082-9	#40 **Claudia and the Middle School Mystery**	$2.95
❑ MG43570-1	#41 **Mary Anne Versus Logan**	$2.95
❑ MG44083-7	#42 **Jessi and the Dance School Phantom**	$2.95
❑ MG43572-8	#43 **Stacey's Emergency**	$2.95
❑ MG43573-6	#44 **Dawn and the Big Sleepover**	$2.95
❑ MG43574-4	#45 **Kristy and the Baby Parade**	$2.95
❑ MG43569-8	#46 **Mary Anne Misses Logan** (August '91)	$2.95
❑ MG43576-0	**New York, New York Baby-sitters Club Super Special #6**	$3.50
❑ MG44997-4	**The Baby-sitters Club 1991-92 Student Planner and Datebook**	$7.95
❑ MG44949-4	**The Baby-sitters Club 1992 Calendar** (Aug. '91)	$8.95
❑ MG44783-1	**The Baby-sitters Club Postcard Book**	$4.95

Available wherever you buy books...or use this order form.

Scholastic Inc., P.O. Box 7502, 2931 E. McCarty Street, Jefferson City, MO 65102

Please send me the books I have checked above. I am enclosing $_____
(please add $2.00 to cover shipping and handling). Send check or money order - no
cash or C.O.D.s please.

Name _____

Address _____

City_____ State/Zip _____

Please allow four to six weeks for delivery. Offer good in the U.S. only. Sorry, mail orders are not
available to residents of Canada. Prices subject to change.

You're not ready for school until you have

THE NEW

BABY-SITTERS CLUB®

1991-92 Student Planner and Date Book!

By Ann M. Martin

Plan for a GREAT school year
with the NEW edition of
**The Baby-sitters Club 1991-92
Student Planner and Date Book!**
It's better than ever, with 144 pages of
EVERYTHING you need for school days and EVERY
day as well as messages, tips, recipes and more
from Kristy, Claudia, Mary Anne, Stacey
and the rest of the gang!

**Available in July wherever you buy
Baby-sitters Club books!**

Planner is 8 1/2" x 11".   BSC1190

THE BABY-SITTERS CLUB®

Vote for your favorite Baby-sitter and...

Win Your Very Own Baby-sitters Club Party!

ONE GRAND PRIZE WINNER RECEIVES:

- A Baby-sitters Club party with Ann M. Martin as Guest of Honor-- complete with food, games, and we'll even videotape the party!
- Baby-sitters Club freebies for ten friends--games, t-shirts, videos, autographed books and more!

Just fill out the coupon below and return it by October 31, 1991.

25 SECOND-PRIZE WINNERS get Baby-sitters Club games!
10 THIRD-PRIZE WINNERS get Baby-sitters Club dolls!

Rules: Entries must be postmarked by October 31, 1991. Winners will be picked at random and notified by mail. No purchase necessary. Valid only in the U.S. and Canada. Void where prohibited. Taxes on prizes are the responsibility of the winners and their immediate families. Employees of Scholastic Inc.; its agencies, affiliates, subsidiaries; and their immediate families are not eligible. For a complete list of winners, send a self-addressed stamped envelope to Vote for Your Favorite Baby-sitter Winners List, at the address provided below.

Check off the name of your favorite Baby-sitter and fill in the coupon below or write the information on a 3" x 5" piece of paper, and mail to: VOTE FOR YOUR FAVORITE BABY-SITTER, P.O. Box 7500, Jefferson City, MO 65102. Canadian residents send entries to: Iris Ferguson, Scholastic Inc., 123 Newkirk Road, Richmond Hill, Ontario, Canada L4C365.

Vote for Your Favorite Baby-sitter!

Who's your favorite Baby-sitter?

- ☐ Kristy Thomas, President
- ☐ Claudia Kishi, Vice-President
- ☐ Mary Anne Spier, Secretary
- ☐ Stacey McGill, Treasurer
- ☐ Dawn Schafer, Alternate Officer
- ☐ Mallory Pike, Junior Officer
- ☐ Jessica Ramsey, Junior Officer

Name_____Age_____

Street_____

City_____State_____Zip_____

Where did you buy this Baby-sitters Club book?

- ☐ Bookstore
- ☐ Library
- ☐ Other_____(specify)
- ☐ Drugstore
- ☐ Book Club
- ☐ Supermarket
- ☐ Book Fair

P.S. Please put your favorite Baby-sitter's name on the outside of your envelope, too! Thanks!

BSC1190

"WHODUNIT?"

FIND OUT IN

THE BABY-SITTERS CLUB®

NEW MYSTERY SERIES!

READ THESE NEW MYSTERIES ALONG WITH YOUR FAVORITE BABY-SITTERS CLUB BOOKS!

Something mysterious *is* going on in Stoneybrook, and now you can solve the case with the Baby-sitters!

A valuable ring disappears...and Stacey is blamed. Can she clear her name before the Baby-sitters lose all their business?

Start Your Collection With The 1ST Exciting Baby-Sitters Club Mystery Book!

STACEY AND THE MISSING RING
By Ann M. Martin

Coming in August wherever you buy *Baby-sitters Club* books!

BSC1290

Baby-sitters Club Fans, It's back...

THE BABY-SITTERS CLUB®

1992 Calendar!

Don't start the new year without **The Baby-sitters Club 1992 Calendar!** Check out all the great new stuff this year's calendar has:

- Two full pages of brand new stickers!
- Portraits of all the Baby-sitters with Stoneybrook kids!
- New full-color illustrations!
- A wipe-off memo board to reuse again and again!

Coming August 1991!

Available wherever you buy Baby-sitters Club books!

Calendar is 10 1/2" x 12."

BSC191

Invite a "Little Sister" to join the

BABY·SITTERS

Little Sister™

Birthday Club!

Do you know a Baby-sitters Little Sister fan? Pass along this page and she can join the **Baby-sitters Little Sister Birthday Club**! Then on her birthday, she'll receive a personalized card from Karen herself!

That's not all! Every month, a **BIRTHDAY KID OF THE MONTH** will be randomly chosen to **WIN** a complete set of *Baby-sitters Little Sister* books! The first book in the set will be autographed by author Ann M. Martin!

Fill in the coupon or write the information on a 3" x 5" piece of paper and mail to:
BABY-SITTERS LITTLE SISTER BIRTHDAY CLUB, Scholastic Inc.,
730 Broadway, P.O. Box 742, New York, New York 10003.
Offer expires March 31, 1992.

- -

Baby-sitters Little Sister Birthday Club

❏ **YES!** I want to join the BABY-SITTERS LITTLE SISTER BIRTHDAY CLUB!

My birthday is_____.

Name_____ Age_____

Street _____
        —

City_____State_____ Zip_____
P.S. Please put your birthday on the *outside* of your envelope too! Thanks!

Where did you buy this book?

❏ Bookstore ❏ Drugstore ❏ Supermarket ❏ Library
❏ Book Club ❏ Book Fair ❏ Other_____(specify)

BSC990